PLANE TALK

Compiled by Carl R. Oliver

PLANE TALK

AVIATORS' AND ASTRONAUTS'

OWN STORIES

Illustrated with photographs

Houghton Mifflin Company Boston 1980

629.13
Pla

Library of Congress Cataloging in Publication Data

Main entry under title:

Plane talk.

Bibliography: p.
1. Air pilots — Biography. 2. Astronauts — Biography.
I. Oliver, Carl R.
TL539.P58   629.13'092'2 [B]   80-16052
ISBN 0-395-29743-5

Copyright acknowledgments appear on pages 177–179

M 10 9 8 7 6 5 4 3 2 1

Contents

PLANE TALK

Preface: The Thrill of Flying

The "thrill of flying"—what is it? John Gillespie Magee, Jr., a pilot, unquestionably captured some of the thrill in this sonnet, written in 1941. Year after year it remains popular with aviators and it adorns the walls of countless crew rooms and flight offices:

High Flight

Oh! I have slipped the surly bonds of Earth
And danced the skies on laughter-silvered wings;
Sunward I've climbed, and joined the tumbling mirth
Of sun-split clouds,—and done a hundred things
You have not dreamed of—wheeled and soared and swung
High in the sunlit silence. Hov'ring there,
I've chased the shouting wind along, and flung
My eager craft through footless halls of air . . .

Up, up the long, delirious, burning blue
I've topped the wind-swept heights with easy grace
Where never lark, or even eagle flew—
And, while with silent, lifting mind I've trod
The high untrespassed sanctity of space,
Put out my hand, and touched the face of God.

Other American aviators have written about the thrill of flying, too. Collected here are a number of their stories— famous pilots talking firsthand about their famous flights. From Orville Wright to astronaut "Buzz" Aldrin, all seem to marvel that minds and hands of Man can create a machine that will soar high into the blue.

Pilot Officer John Gillespie Magee, Jr. (*Canadian Forces*)

1. Orville Wright
on Inventing the Airplane

Our first interest [in flying] began when we were children. Father brought home to us a small toy actuated by a rubber spring which would lift itself into the air.

In the spring of 1899 our interest in the subject was again aroused. We could not understand that there was anything about a bird that would enable it to fly that could not be built on a larger scale and used by man.

We were much impressed with the great number of people who had given thought to it—among these some of the greatest minds the world has produced. But we found that the experiments of one after another had failed.

We found that [Otto] Lilienthal had been killed through his inability to properly balance his machine in the air. Pilcher, an English experimenter, had met with a like fate. We found that both of these experimenters had attempted to maintain balance merely by the shifting of the weight of their bodies. We at once set to work to devise a more efficient means of maintaining the equilibrium.

From the tables of Lilienthal we calculated that a machine having an area of a little over 150 square feet would support a man when flown in a wind of 16 miles an hour. We attempted to fly the machine as a kite with a man on board a number of times, but were successful in keeping it up only when the wind was about 25 miles or more an hour. Measurements show[ed] a lift of about one-third of the estimates that had been made using the Lilienthal tables of air pressure.

All the books and papers taught that the center of pressure was approximately at the center of the surface when it was exposed at right angles to the wind [and] moved forward as the angle of incidence was decreased. We had built both the 1900 and 1901 machines assuming this to be well verified. Our elevator was placed in front of the surfaces with the idea of producing inherent stability fore and aft, which it should have done had the travel of the center of pressure been forward as we had been led to believe. We found, however, that

Orville (left) and Wilbur Wright in 1897. (*Library of Congress*)

these machines were anything but inherently stable fore and aft.

Our experiments of 1901 were rather discouraging to us because we felt that they demonstrated that some of the most firmly established laws, those regarding the travel of the center of pressure and pressures on airplane surfaces, were mostly, if not entirely, incorrect.

In September we set up a small wind tunnel in which we made a number of measurements. We also designed and constructed another instrument for measuring the ratio of the lift to the drift. We decided to build another machine, basing it upon calculations to be made from our own tables.

We went to Kitty Hawk in the last week of August 1902 and began the assembling of a machine embodying the changes. The [unpowered] flights of 1902 demonstrated the efficiency of our systems of control for both longitudinal and lateral stability. They also demonstrated that our tables of air pressure which we made in our wind tunnel would enable us to calculate in advance the performance of a machine.

Immediately after our return from Kitty Hawk in 1902 we wrote to a number of the best-known automobile manufacturers in an endeavor to secure a motor for the new machine. Not receiving favorable answers from any of these, we proceeded to design a motor of our own.

We designed the propellers which we used in this 1903 machine. These propellers had an efficiency of over 66 percent, an efficiency, I believe, never approached by any of the aeronautical investigators up to that time.

We went to Kitty Hawk the latter part of September 1903. The first attempt to fly this machine was made on the 14th of December, but through a mistake in handling it at the start, the machine was broken slightly, so that repairs had to be made.

3

Orville Wright at controls, Wilbur afoot. (*Library of Congress*)

The next trial was on the 17th of December. In a wind blowing 20 miles [per hour] and more, four flights were made. The first of these flights was the first time in the history of the world that a machine carrying a man and driven by a motor had lifted itself from the ground in free flight.

The first flight covered a distance of a little more than 100 feet over the ground, against a wind of nearly 25 miles an hour. As a result of the gustiness of the wind, and the inexperience of the operator, the machine traveled over an undulating course, sometimes 10 feet from the ground and sometimes not more than a foot or two. The time of this flight was about 12 seconds. The second flight covered a distance of about 175 feet over the ground. The third flight was slightly longer than the second, and the fourth flight covered a distance of 852 feet measured over the ground, and had a duration of 59 seconds. The height of all of these flights ranged from a few feet to 12 to 15 feet above the ground.

2. Benjamin D. Foulois on Flying Cross-country with Orville Wright

On December 23, 1907, General [James] Allen signed Signal Corps Specification No. 486 for a heavier-than-air flying machine, asking for sealed proposals to be received by noon of February 1, 1908.

The airplane had to be designed "so that it may be quickly and easily assembled and taken apart and packed for transportation in army wagons." It had to be able to carry two people having a combined weight of about 350 pounds and enough gasoline for a 125-mile flight. A speed of 40 miles per hour was to be averaged, with a bonus of 10 percent for each mile above that speed up to 44 miles per hour and penalties of 10 percent for each mile per hour less than 40.

In addition, a one-hour endurance flight was required, and the airplane "shall return to the starting point and land without any damage that would prevent its immediately starting upon another flight."

5

I was assigned to the office of the Chief Signal Officer of the Army in July [1908], and placed in charge of the Balloon Detachment at Fort Myer, Virginia.

Orville and Wilbur [Wright came] to Washington on June 20 [1909]. It took a month for the Wrights to assemble the machine and test-fly it until they were satisfied with its performance. I hung around them every day and pestered them with questions based on what I had read. Finally, Wilbur stopped working after I had put a question to him, and asked, "What in the world have you been reading to ask something like that?"

"Everything I can lay my hands on," I replied.

Obviously exasperated, Wilbur said, "There are no books worth reading on the subject of flying. You get your hands on that machine over there if you really want to learn about it."

This was a rare invitation for the Wrights to extend to anyone, and I was delighted. I donned my coveralls, stuck a pair of pliers, a screw driver, cotton waste, and a bar of soap in my pockets, and got to work.

Close-mouthed and quiet, the only thing the Wrights liked to discuss was their machine and the forthcoming tests. Orville was the more talkative of the two, which wasn't saying much. He was amiable and kind-faced. Wilbur, prematurely bald, about forty then, had deeper furrows in his face and seemed to look at you with a kind of reserved suspicion. When you spoke to the two of them, it would be Orville who would answer, and Wilbur would either nod his assent or add an incomplete sentence as his way of corroborating what his younger brother had said.

After a number of short flights, Orville made an endurance flight of one hour, twenty minutes, on July 20. On the 27th, with [Lieutenant] Frank Lahm as passenger, he flew one hour,

Wilbur Wright, Benjamin Foulois, Orville Wright. (*U.S. Air Force*)

twelve minutes, and forty seconds, thus more than fulfilling the requirement to remain in the air for an hour with a passenger.

Next and last specification to be satisfied was the speed test over a measured 5-mile course. Because of my previous mapmaking experience, Major [George O.] Squier asked me to lay out the course.

I chose a rise of ground at Alexandria, Virginia, almost due south of Fort Myer, called Shooter's Hill, to be used as a turning point. I chose this site because it was above the surrounding terrain and should have been easy to navigate toward at an altitude of 100 or so feet.

Remembering my dirigible experience, I was concerned that we would wander off our course from Myer to Alexandria, so I arranged for a small captive balloon to be ascended from Shooter's Hill and one anchored about halfway between the two points.

The only question was who was to be the navigator-passenger on this all-important flight. It was decided that the Wrights should make their choice. They did: me.

I would like to think that I was chosen on the basis of my intellectual and technical ability, but I found out later that it was my short stature, light weight, and map-reading experience that had tipped the decision in my favor.

About 7000 people showed up on the afternoon of July 30. About four o'clock it looked as though the sky was clearing and the wind was dying down.

The Wrights pushed their machine to the starting rail and made many adjustments to the engine and guy wires. I put two stopwatches around my neck and got into the passenger seat. I strapped a box compass to my left thigh, lashed an aneroid barometer to my right thigh, and jammed a map into my belt.

Orville warmed up the engine until he was satisfied with it, and climbed aboard. "If I have any trouble," he shouted above the roar of the engine, "I'll land in a field or the thickest clump of trees I can find."

I nodded and gulped. I had picked a course with no fields of any kind en route. It was too late to do anything about it now, so I grabbed the edge of the seat with both hands and

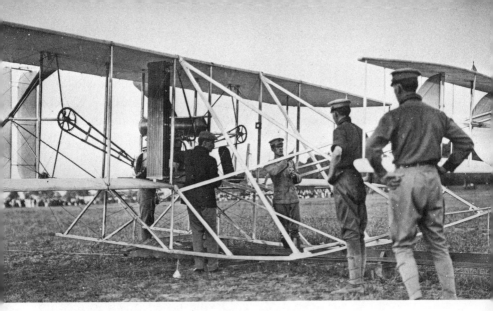

Orville Wright readies aircraft. (*U.S. Air Force*)

waited. Orville revved up the engine, released the trigger, and the machine started down the rail.

We skimmed over the grass for a few feet to gain speed, and then climbed for altitude. As we started to circle, Wilbur ran to the center of the field below us with a stopwatch in one hand and a signal flag in the other. We made two complete circles of the field, gaining altitude (125 feet), and then Orville swung sharply over the starting line. I flicked one stopwatch and pointed out the exact course we should follow to Shooter's Hill.

All 25 horses in the engine were functioning perfectly as we skimmed over the tree tops toward the first balloon. The air was bumpy, and I had the feeling that there were moments when Orville didn't have full control of the machine as we dipped groundward. It was as if someone on the ground had a string attached to us and would pull it occasionally, as they would a kite. But each time Orville would raise the elevators slightly, and we would gain back the lost altitude.

We reached Shooter's Hill all right, and I flicked the second stopwatch. There was a crowd on the brow of the hill, and I could see them wave their umbrellas and handkerchiefs. It seemed to me that the angle of bank of the plane was awfully steep as we rounded the turn and the wing tip was much too close to the tops of the trees. A down draft hit us, and I thought we were going to cartwheel into them for sure. We straightened out, however, and started back for Myer.

Going downwind now, our ground speed increased and Orville climbed until we reached 400 feet—a world's altitude record. As we neared Myer, Orville nosed down to pick up speed, and aimed at the starting tower. I flicked the stopwatch off as we crossed the starting line and relaxed as he made a circle over Arlington Cemetery, cut off the engine, and glided in for a fairly smooth landing amid a cloud of dust.

Wilbur rushed up to us, and it was the first time I ever saw him with a smile on his face. President Taft had not been present for the takeoff but had seen us land, and sent a messenger through the crowds to us with a note of congratulation.

As soon as the board members could get together, we compared our stopwatches and determined that the official speed to Alexandria had been 37.735 miles per hour; on the return trip it was calculated at 47.431 miles per hour, with the average officially computed at 42.583 miles per hour.

On August 2, 1909, Aeroplane No. 1 was officially accepted into the inventory of the United States Army.

3. Henry H. (Hap) Arnold on Learning to Fly at the Wright Company

Out of the blue an official letter arrived from the War Department. Would I be willing to volunteer for training with the Wright brothers at Dayton [Ohio] as an airplane pilot?

Puzzled, I took the letter to my commanding officer. After reading it, he said, "Young man, I know of no better way for a person to commit suicide!" It was a challenge.

Thus it was that on a night in the third week of April 1911, I found myself on a train bound from New York to Dayton. In my pocket was a copy of War Department Special Order 95, dated 21 April, 1911. In accordance with paragraph 10,

> The following named officers are detailed for aeronautical duty with the Signal Corps, and will proceed to Dayton, Ohio, for the purpose of undergoing a course of instruction in operating the Wright airplane:

2nd Lt. Henry H. Arnold, 29th Infantry
2nd Lt. Thomas DeW. Milling, 15th Cavalry

The travel directed is necessary in the military service.

Back in the early 1900s, when the area surrounding Dayton, Ohio, was not so thickly populated as it is today, there were many small farms—one in particular located about 9 miles out of town at a place called Simms Station. Later, it was sometimes called Huffman Field after the well-to-do citizen who had allowed the Wright brothers to use it free of charge for their experiments. It was a cow pasture, not very different from hundreds of other fields in the vicinity. It had a large thorn tree at one end, and at the other end a fairly large wooden shed. The balance of the field was clear of trees and bushes.

When I arrived at Dayton I went first to the Wright factory, not to "the field." There was nobody at Simms Station except, perhaps, a mechanic working on one of the two planes, because it was only in the early morning or in the evening that one could try to go up—the rest of the time there was too much wind.

Wilbur and Orville Wright, as well as Frank Russel, who was the first person I met in the corridor of the factory, gave me a warm welcome.

Milling and I were soon grateful for the days spent in the factory, for in addition to learning how to fly we found we would have to master the construction and maintenance features of the Wright machine well enough to teach our own mechanics the ABC of a ground crew's job when we went to our first station.

Our primary training also took place in the factory. Almost

Final assembly at the Wright Company. (*U.S. Air Force*)

as soon as we arrived, Orville and Wilbur Wright, Cliff Turpin, who was to be Milling's instructor, and Al Welsh, who was mine, took us out to a back room of the shop where an old plane was balanced on sawhorse supports so that the wing tips could move up and down.

In the Wright plane, after crawling under wires which crossed in front, one sat on a hard seat located on the leading edge of the thin lower wing. The airman's feet rested on a slender bar before the wing. For the elevator, the Wright pilot moved a vertical stick in the conventional manner of the present type of control. There were two of these sticks, one outside each seat, for whichever pilot happened to be flying the plane, but there were not two complete sets of controls. The third stick, between the two aviators, though it also moved fore and aft, was for lateral balance and rudder. The top portion of this middle lever was hinged to rock laterally, and was connected by a rod to a quadrant on the same shaft as the warp control. The rudder could be moved either in combination with the warping or independently. (Today, of course, ailerons are used in lieu of the twisting of the wings.)

A right turn, for example, was achieved by pulling the lever back to lift the left wing and simultaneously rotating the hand grip an appropriate number of degrees to the right for right rudder. After the turn was started, the pilot eased back to normal attitude for level flying. This scarcely instinctive procedure had to be mastered before one could go into the air as a Wright pilot. The old plane mounted on a sawhorse was how you began.

The lateral controls were connected with small clutches at the wing tips, and grabbed a moving belt running over a pulley. A forward motion, and the clutch would snatch the belt, and down would go the left wing. A backward pull, and the reverse would happen. The jolts and teetering were so violent that the student was kept busy just moving the lever back and forth to keep on an even keel. That was primary training and it lasted for days; in the meantime, actual flying instruction was received in an airplane out at Simms Station.

I still have the official summary which Al Welsh turned in

Wright model B. (*U.S. Air Force*)

Al Welsh and Hap Arnold at Simms Station, 1911. (*U.S. Air Force*)

to the Wright Company on my training. The first date is May 3, 1911. In the line reporting Lesson No. 1, Al notes that the flight lasted 7 minutes, and that he carried Lieutenant Arnold as a pupil. "Rough," he says under "Remarks," "just rode as passenger."

The next lesson lasted only five minutes; the "Remarks" were the same. But the day following, with twelve minutes in the air, my first operational experience was described, "Hand on elevator." Lesson No. 4, and I "had charge of elevator part of the time." Then four more tries, each lasting from seven to fourteen minutes, and Welsh could report that during Lesson No. 9 I "Had charge of warping lever part of the time." After flight No. 10—really two hops lasting fourteen and three minutes—there is the notation, "To Shed." I had taxied the plane myself.

Beginning with Lesson No. 12, Al was "teaching landing." And Lieutenant Arnold, at Lesson No. 19, "Landed without assistance" and "To Shed." The flights that day were four minutes and one minute long, respectively. Thereafter, it went rapidly. Following five minutes in the air on Lesson No. 26, I "landed without assistance," and as we came in from Lesson No. 28, I again triumphantly "Landed without assistance." I could fly! I was an aviator!

Al wrote at the bottom of my report, "Number of flights, 28. Total time in air 3 hours 48 minutes. First lesson 3 May, finished 13 May—10 days learning. Average 8 minutes." (The actual elapsed time was eleven days, since the Wrights didn't fly on the Sabbath.) Al signed it "A. L. Welsh, Teacher," and turned it in. He had taught me all he knew. Or, rather, he had taught me all he could *teach*. He knew much more.

All those early aviators knew more than they could tell anybody. But what was it they knew, or knew they didn't know? Things happened, that was all. The air was a tricky place. The best laws, discovered and formulated by the best aeronautical brains, could still be upset, it seemed, in a second. "It" could still happen to anybody's plane. Well, not "anybody's," of course. Despite the serious, mysterious talk of "holes in the air," and so on, the personal factor was continuously stressed. If Joe crashed, he must have done something that you would never do. You and the other flyers talked it over and eventually "decided" what it was. The fact that one of your own number presently joined the casualty list did not alter this dogged credo. *He* had done something else, now, that none of the rest of you would do. It is interesting that in that day, when there was none of our modern standardization of planes, controls, or flying equipment, it was seldom the plane, or an unknown quantity in the air, but almost always the pilot, who was blamed for being in error. You *had* to believe that to keep up your morale.

In those days, the primitive method for determining whether the engine was turning up fast enough seemed satisfactory. You just used a revolution counter on the propeller shaft, and took time with a stopwatch. If you wanted to be really scientific about testing the engine, the flying machine was hitched to a rope, the rope to a spring balance, and it, in turn, was tied to a stake in the ground. Then, by reading the scale on the spring balance with the engine running full-out, you determined the actual propeller thrust.

The only instrument used on airplanes when I began to fly was a piece of string tied to the front crossbar on the skids. When it stood out directly to the rear, everything was O.K. —the pilot was flying correctly. When it drifted to one side or the other, the plane was in a skid. That piece of string was a wonderful instrument.

The safety belt came along as an airplane accessory by accident. The then Lieutenant—now Admiral—Jack Towers was thrown from his seat on an old Wright plane. The pilot, Lieutenant Billingsly, was tossed clear; since he had no parachute, he didn't have a chance, and dropped like a rock into the ocean. Towers, rattling around between wings, struts, and wires, managed finally to grab a wire and hang on until the plane hit the water. He remained conscious, lashed himself to a pontoon with his belt, and was picked up soon afterward. Subsequently, he spent several weeks in a hospital. After that, we all used safety belts, and Milling devised an improved version which is practically the one in use today.

The first goggles worn by Army airmen came as the result of a bug's hitting me in the eye as I was landing my plane.

Prior to that time, our custom was simple. We merely turned our caps backward and were all dressed to sit on the lower wing and start flying. On this particular flight, soon after I left Simms Station, I was coming back into the field when a bug hit me in the eye and left one of its transparent wings sticking to my eyeball. The pain was terrific; blinded by tears I could scarcely see to make my landing. As a matter of fact, it was some days before the doctors were able to find that transparent wing and remove it. The possibility of being rammed dead by a bug had not occurred to us before. After that we wore goggles.

4. Edward V. Rickenbacker on Overcoming the Weaknesses of Aircraft

[On May 2, 1918] Lieutenant Jimmy Meissner of Brooklyn had [a] very trying experience with the Nieuport machine. About noon he and Lieutenant Davis were sent out to protect a French observation machine which had been ordered to take photographs of the enemy's positions back of Pont-à-Mousson. The photography machine went down to seven or eight thousand feet and was proceeding calmly on its work, leaving the matter of its defense to the two American pilots sitting upstairs some four or five thousand feet overhead.

Suddenly Jimmy Meissner discovered two Albatros fighting machines almost upon him, coming from out of the sun. They were already on the attack and were firing as they dived swiftly upon the two Nieuports.

Jimmy made a quick maneuver and zoomed up above the nearest Albatros. Instantly he utilized his advantage, now that he had the upper floor, and in a trice he headed downward upon the tail of the enemy, firing long bursts from his machine gun as he plunged after the fleeing Hun. But the Albatros pilot was an old hand at this game, and before Meissner could overtake him he had thrown his machine into a tailspin which not only presented a target difficult to hit, but almost persuaded Jimmy that the machine was falling out of control.

Jimmy had heard many stories of this sort of "playing possum" however. He determined to keep after the spinning Albatros and see the end of the combat. Accordingly he opened his throttle and dived headlong down. One thousand, two thousand, three thousand feet he plunged, regardless of everything but the occasional target that whirled periodically before his sights. At last he got in a burst that produced immediate results. The Albatros sent out a quick puff of smoke that was immediately followed by a mass of flames. One of Meissner's tracer bullets had set fire to the fuel tank of the enemy's machine. The plucky victor pulled up his Nieuport and took a self-satisfied look about him.

There scarcely a thousand feet below him were the enemy's lines. From various directions machine guns and Archies [antiaircraft guns] were directing their fire upon him. He grinned at them contemptuously and looked away for the expected view of Lieutenant Davis' Nieuport and the other Albatros. Neither was to be seen. Perhaps they were on his other wing. One glance around to the left and Jimmy's heart was in his throat.

He saw that the entire length of his left upper wing was stripped of fabric! And as he turned a horrified gaze to the other wing, he saw that its fabric too was even at that moment beginning to tear away from its leading edge and was flapping in the wind! So furious had been his downward plunge that the force of the wind's pressure had torn away the fragile covering on both his upper wings. Without this supporting surface his airplane would drop like a stone. Although it couldn't make much difference whether it dropped into German lines or within his own so far as his life was concerned, Meissner admitted later he always wanted a military funeral; so he eased off his speed and tenderly turned about his wobbling machine and headed back toward France.

Giving the slightest possible engine power and nursing his crippled little 'bus with great delicacy, Meissner succeeded in gaining No Man's Land, then passed over the American trenches. He did not dare to alter either his direction or speed. Less than half a mile farther his machine glided into the earth and crashed beyond repair. Meissner crawled from the wreckage and felt himself all over carefully, to try to make himself understand that he was in reality in the land of the living—and free.

[On May 7, 1918] I ran over to [Lieutenant Eddie] Green to inquire for news of [Captain] Jimmy [Hall]. My heart was heavy within me, for I was certain what the answer would be.

"Went down in a tailspin with his upper wing gone!" Green informed me without my speaking. "I saw him dive onto a Boche just as I began my attack. The next I saw of him, he was going in a spin and the Boche was still firing at him as he was falling. He must have struck just back of those woods behind Montsec."

I cannot describe the joy that came to the squadron about a month later when we received a letter from Jimmy Hall himself. He wrote from a hospital in Germany, where he was laid up with a broken ankle. He had not been shot down in the combat, as we had supposed, but had dived too swiftly for the weak wing structure of a Nieuport. His upper wing had collapsed in full flight; and not until he had almost reached the ground had he been able to straighten out his airplane. In the crash he had escaped with merely a cracked ankle.

[On May 17, 1918] I noticed three graceful Albatros machines leave the ground one after the other. It was evident from their straightaway course that they were going over the lines, gaining their altitude as they flew southward. I made myself as inconspicuous as possible until the last of the three had his back well toward me. Then I returned to my course and gradually narrowed the distance between us.

By the time we reached Montsec, that celebrated mountain north of Saint-Mihiel, I estimated some three thousand feet separated me from my unsuspicious quarry. I was so eager to let them get over our lines before attacking that I quite forgot I was now a conspicuous figure to the German Archies. Two quick bursts just ahead of me informed me of my error. Without waiting to see whether or not I was hit, I put on the sauce and dived down headlong at the rearmost of the three Huns.

I saw the warning signal sent up ahead of the three Albatros pilots. A single black burst from the battery below caused the German airmen to turn about and look behind them. They had not expected any attack from this quarter.

When the leader made the first swerve aside I was less than 200 yards from the rear Albatros. I was descending at a furious pace, regardless of everything but my target ahead. Fully 200 miles an hour my Nieuport was flying. Without checking her speed, I kept her nose pointing at the tail of the rear Albatros, which was now darting steeply downward to escape me. As the distance closed to 50 yards I saw my tracer bullets piercing the back of the pilot's seat. I had been firing for perhaps ten seconds from first to last. The scared Boche had made the mistake of trying to outdive me instead of outmaneuvering me. He paid for his blunder with his life.

Eddie Rickenbacker with Nieuport, May 5, 1918. (*National Archives*)

These thoughts flashed through my mind in the fraction of a moment. All the while my fingers pressed the trigger I was conscious of the danger of my position. Either or both of the other enemy machines were undoubtedly now on my tail, exactly as I had been on their unfortunate companion. And being alone I must rely solely upon my own maneuvers to escape them.

I believe I should have followed my first target all the way to the ground regardless of the consequences, so desperately had I determined to get him. So I perhaps prolonged my terrific speed a trifle too long. As the enemy airplane fell off and began to flutter I pulled my stick back close into my lap and began a sharp climb. A frightening crash that sounded like the crack of doom told me that the sudden strain had collapsed my right wing. The entire spread of canvas over the top wing was torn off by the wind and disappeared behind me. Deprived of any supporting surface on this framework, the Nieuport turned over on her right side. The tail was forced up despite all my efforts with joystick and rudder. Slowly at first, then faster and faster, the tail began revolving around and around. Swifter and swifter became our downward speed. I was caught in a *vrille,* or tailspin, and with a machine as crippled as mine there seemed not a chance to come out of it.

I wondered vaguely whether the two Albatros machines would continue to fire at me all the way down. Twice I watched them dive straight at me firing more bullets into my helpless little craft, notwithstanding the apparent certainty of her doom. I felt no anger toward them. I felt somewhat critical toward their bad judgment in thus wasting ammunition. No, that was not exactly it either. My senses were getting confused. What I felt critical about was their stupidity in believing I was playing possum. They were fools not to know when an airplane was actually falling to a crash. A great spread of my fabric was gone. No pilot ever could fly without fabric on his machine.

Where would I strike, I wondered. There were the woods

of Montsec below me. Heavens! how much nearer the ground was getting! I wondered if the whole framework of the machine would disintegrate and fling me out to the mercy of the four winds. If I struck in tree tops it was barely possible that I might escape with a score of broken bones. Both Jimmy Meissner and Jimmy Hall had escaped death when betrayed through this same fault of the Nieuport. Never would I fly one again if I once got out of this fix alive! But no use worrying about that now. Either I should not be alive or else I should be a mangled prisoner in Germany. Which would my mother rather have, I wondered.

This sudden longing to see my mother again roused my fighting spirit. With that thought of her and the idea of her opening a cablegram from the front telling her I was dead, with that picture before my mind a whole series of childhood scenes were vividly recalled to me. I have never before realized that one actually does see all the events of one's life pass before one's eyes at the approach of death. Doubtless they are but a few recollections in reality, but one's natural terror at the imminence of death multiplies them into many.

I began to wonder why the speed of my spin did not increase. With every swing around the circle I felt a regular jar as the shock of the air cushion came against the left wing after passing through the right. I felt a growing irritation at these monotonous bumps. But although I had been experimenting constantly with rudder, joystick, and even with the weight of my body I found I was totally unable to modify in the slightest the stubborn spiral gait of the airplane. Fully 10,000 feet I had fallen in this manner since my wing had collapsed. I looked overboard. It was scarcely 3000 feet more—and then the crash! I could see men standing on the road in front of a line of trucks. All were gazing white-faced at me. They were already exulting over the souvenirs they would get from my machine—from my body itself.

With a vicious disregard for consequences, I pulled open the throttle. The sudden extra speed from the engine was too much for the perpendicular tail and before I had realized it the whole fuselage was quite horizontal. Like a flash I seized the joystick and reversed my rudder. The pull of the propeller kept her straight. If only I could keep her so for five minutes I might make the lines. They seemed to beckon to me only two miles or so ahead. I looked above and below.

No airplanes in the sky. My late enemies evidently were sure I was done for. Below me I saw the landscape slipping swiftly behind me. I was making headway much faster than I was falling. Sudden elation began to sweep over me. I boldly tried lifting her head. No use! She would fly straight but that was all. Ah! here comes friend Archie!

It is curious that one gets so accustomed to Archie that its terrors actually disappear. So grateful was I to the crippled little 'bus for not letting me down that I continued to talk to her and promise her a good rubdown when we reached the stable. I hardly realized that Archie was trying to be nasty.

Over the lines I slid, a good thousand feet up. Once freed from the danger of landing in Germany, I tried several small tricks and succeeded in persuading the damaged craft to one more effort. I saw the roofs of my hangar before me. With the engine still running wide open I grazed the tops of the old 94 hangar and pancaked upon my field.

The French pilots from an adjoining hangar came running out to see what novice was trying to make a landing with his engine on. Later they told me I resembled a bird alighting with a broken wing.

The principal fear that hampered me in the midst of a combat was the knowledge that the Nieuport's wings might give way under the stress of a necessary maneuver. Was there no way to strengthen these wings? Why couldn't we get the Spads that had been promised us? If I could only get a machine built according to my own designs!

[On July 5, 1918] the impulse came to me to go down to Orly, where the American Experimental Aerodrome was located, and see for myself just what the situation was in regard to our Spad airplanes. I called upon the major in charge of the Supply Depot, and there learned to my delight that he had actually begun arrangements for the immediate equipment of the Hat-in-the-Ring Squadron with the long-deferred Spads. At that moment, he told me, there were three Spads on the field that were designated for our use.

With a rather short farewell to the major, I hastened to the field. And there I found three of the coveted fighting machines that I knew had many accomplishments superior to the rival Fokkers. The nearest machine to me had the initial figure "I" painted on its sides. I asked the mechanics in charge if this machine had been tested.

Rickenbacker with Spad, October 18, 1918. (*National Archives*)

"Yes, sir! All ready to go to the front!" was the reply.

"Is this one of the machines belonging to 94 Squadron?" I inquired.

"Yes, sir. There are two more over there. The others will be in here in a few days."

"Well, I am down here from 94 Squadron myself," I continued, a sudden wild hope entering my brain. "Is there any reason why this machine should not go to the squadron today?"

"None that I know of, sir!" the mechanic answered, thereby forming a resolution in my mind that I very well knew might lead me to a court-martial, provided my superior officers chose to take a military view of my offense.

Inside ten minutes I was strapped in the seat of the finest little Spad that ever flew French skies. Without seeking further permission or considering stopping to collect my bag at my hotel, I gave the signal to pull away the chocks, sped swiftly across the smooth field, and with a feeling of tremendous satisfaction I headed directly away for the Touquin aerodrome.

Not until I had landed and had begun to answer the questions of my comrades as to how I got possession of the new machine, did I begin to realize the enormity of the offense I had committed. I did not contemplate with any pleasure the questions that the commanding officer would hurl at me, on this subject.

But to my joy no censure was given me. On the contrary I was given this first Spad to use as my own! Within an hour my mechanics were fitting the guns and truing up the wings.

By August 8, 1918, our whole squadron was fitted out with the machines which we had so long coveted. The delight of the pilots can be imagined. In the meantime we had lost a number of pilots on the flimsy Nieuports, not by reason of their breaking up in air but because the pilots who handled them feared to put them into essential maneuvers which they were unable to stand. Consequently our pilots on Nieuports could not always obtain a favorable position over an enemy nor safely escape from a dangerous situation. The Spads were staunch and strong and could easily outdive the Nieuports.

5. Dean C. Smith
on Flying the Mail

What was so dangerous about flying the mail? True, the Air Mail was all cross-country flying, much of it over hilly, rough terrain. True, too, the planes, mostly DH-4's and a few Curtiss R's, all war surplus, had to go in and out of small and unimproved fields instead of military airdromes. Worse, there were only a few mechanics who knew a spark plug from an aileron, and it was about even money that the pilot would have an engine failure on any given flight. But worst of all there was the attitude of the Post Office Department. A pilot had to try to get through regardless of the consequences; he couldn't cancel without giving it a try. Three or four of their pilots, it seemed, had learned to fly some pretty bad weather; and if those pilots could get through, the P.O. brass figured that the others should do the same.

I turned to Pop Anglin. Pop shook his head solemnly. But he gave me the telephone number of D. B. Colyer, manager

Dean C. Smith in 1922. (*National Archives*)

of the Post Office Air Mail Service, which had its headquarters at College Park, outside Washington.

Colyer seemed delighted at the prospect of hiring a pilot. He asked if I could fly a De Havilland. I said I'd never had any trouble with the plane. That was true enough, since I had never flown one. He told me to hustle on down and he would pay the fare.

Even though everyone considered the Air Mail the next thing to suicide, you could at least be comfortable while life lasted. A mail pilot started at $2400 a year; he would get a $200 raise after he logged each 50 hours until he was making $3600. If assigned to multiengined planes like the Martin Bomber, he would get still another $100 a month. This added up to good money. This was my rationalization. Besides, what choice did I have?

College Park seemed a most unpretentious show to be the headquarters of the Air Mail Service. There were three or four shackline wooden hangars, a hut for an office, and an exceedingly small, badly rolling, sod field. I was yet to learn that this was a sumptuous airdrome as compared with the typical Air Mail field. I located D. B. Colyer. As soon as the southbound got in, he told me, the pilot would check me out in a Jenny. If he gave me an O.K., they would put me in a DH, and see what I could do. And if I then got down in one piece, I would be in business. A mechanic showed me the layout, as I quizzed him anxiously about the switches and valves on the DH.

The incoming pilot took little time to check me out. He hustled me into the front seat of the Curtiss trainer, had me take off, make a quick circle of the field, and land. That was all. He gave Colyer a breezy O.K. and was off.

The De Havilland was a challenge, more psychological than actual, but enough to make me nervous as I climbed in for my first flight. When I was introduced to the JN-4 I had been impressed with the throb of its 90-horsepower engine. The DH had a Liberty engine of 400 horsepower; its roar made the ground shake. But the mechanic's lesson proved invaluable, and I carefully followed his instructions. Once clear, I taxied to the corner, pointed the plane the long way of the field, and gave her the gun before I had time to change my mind. The plane took off easily. After a few maneuvers I knew I was flying the plane instead of the plane flying me, and I started getting a boot out of it.

There was an exhilaration to flying an airplane in those days: their slow speed and light wing-loadings allowed short turns, sharp dives, and quick pull-outs that are impossible in faster planes. We did not rely on gauges and indicators; we flew by feel, noting the control pressures on our hands and feet, the shifting weight of our bodies, and the pitch of the singing wires. I was careful with my first few landings, bringing the DH in flat, with a bit of power until I got over the fence. After a dozen landings I taxied in to find I had become a mail pilot. This was in April 1920.

After several days at College Park, I was given a permanent assignment based at Bellefonte, Pennsylvania, whence I was to fly to Cleveland. Bellefonte lies at the heart of the Allegheny Mountains, in central Pennsylvania. I checked in with a Mr. Tanner, the field manager, and asked him what I was to do. So far as he knew, he said, I had only to fly back and forth to Cleveland. Never having been to Cleveland, I asked him for maps. He smiled. There were no maps. Sometimes on his first trip a pilot would fly behind someone who knew the run.

When Max Miller, the senior pilot of the whole Air Mail Service, showed up, I asked him how to get started. Rand McNally road maps, he explained, were useful, but they didn't show the landmarks I would use most in flying the run, such as the shape and layout of the towns, the distinctive appearance of the hills and valleys, where the low places were that let you work your way through weather, and the location of possible landing fields. After I came to know my run, Miller said, I'd fly to Cleveland the way I'd walk to the drugstore; I'd know the way.

Miller and I picked up maps of Pennsylvania and Ohio. Then he began to talk. He kept on talking for a long time. From the field here at Bellefonte you head west through the gap in the ridge. Climb as you veer a bit north, passing over the center of this railroad switchback up the side of Rattlesnake Mountain, then due west again to clear the top of the ridge at, say, 2200 feet. After about 10 miles you hit the railroad again at Snow Shoe—look sharp, it's only four or five houses—then follow the railroad on down the other side of Rattlesnake to the valley where you pick up the West Branch of the Susquehanna River, winding along to the town of Clearfield, which you will know by three round water reservoirs just south of town. Next, you have to get over about 30 miles of plateau to Du Bois. This is pretty high, about 2200 feet, but it is fairly smooth on top and there is a white gravel road cut

Mail delivery at Bellefonte Station. (*Library of Congress*)

through the trees straight to Du Bois. As you come into town you will see the railroad to your right and just south of the railroad a piece of flat pasture you can land on in a pinch. Then the highway leads you for 50 miles through Brookville to Clarion. Each of these towns has a half-mile race track. The one at Clarion is half full of trees, but the one at Brookville is clean and hard, and it's the best emergency field from here to Cleveland: as soon as you land you will be met by a girl named Alice Henderson, driving a big Cadillac, who will be pleased to look after you. After Clarion, the country gradually gets lower until you cross the Allegheny at Greenville, which you can identify by a big S bend in the river. From then on it's clear sailing.

And so he went on, naming towns, hills, rivers, roads, factories, race tracks, all the way to Cleveland. The airfield was in East Cleveland, at the Glenn L. Martin plant. It was easy to find, just a quarter of a mile from the lake shore—or so Miller assured me.

I had expected to make my first trip escorted by one of the Cleveland pilots. But within a few days the westbound came in and there was no pilot except me available to take it on to Cleveland. The weather was far from promising; it had been raining off and on all day, and low clouds were barely clearing the ridges. However, no one seemed concerned as they transferred the mail to my DH and warmed up the Liberty, so I took off and headed west through the gap in the first ridge. Max's instructions proved a great help. I made it over Rattlesnake Mountain and followed the river to Clearfield without much trouble. Opaque veils of cloud forced me to twist and dodge my way between them as the squalls grew heavier. By the time I reached the slope leading up to the plateau, the clouds were so solid that I had to circle back. I hated to give

35

up. Over Clearfield again the sky looked brighter to the north, so I blithely headed that way, happily ignorant that I was flying over some of the wildest country in Pennsylvania, high and rugged, with few houses and no fields for 50 miles around.

I was able to work my way west by heading for openings between the clouds, zigzagging from one to another. I knew I was north of the course, but not how far north; I knew I was working west, but I couldn't guess at what rate. I was amazed to find I was barely clearing the trees, although the altimeter showed close to 3000 feet above sea level. The terrain was rushing at me with relentless speed. After a long half hour, the rain eased a bit and the clouds rose. I relaxed a little. I was showing them that a rookie could get through.

Just then, the engine stopped cold. As a rule when an engine fails, it will give some warning. The water temperature will rise, or the oil pressure will drop, or there's a knocking or clanking. Even if it is only a minute or two, it gives the pilot a chance to look around and head for a field or open place. However, when the timing gear in a Liberty engine fails, one second it is roaring along even and strong, and the next there is a tremendous, loud silence. I quickly twisted all the knobs and gadgets in the cockpit, but there was no response and the engine stayed dead. While my hands were trying to restart the engine, my neck was stretching and my eyes searching for some sort of field to land in. I was surrounded by heavily forested, sharply rolling hills. To my left was a cuplike basin with a small clearing. It was downwind, but my gliding radius didn't allow much choice. I went for it.

To reach the clearing required a sharp, almost vertical S turn, first left, then right, while killing just enough speed and altitude to land, downwind, and still miss a nearby cliff. I can even now feel the rain slanting in my face and see that open space rocking and swinging in front of me as I pulled out of the turn. One thing I could not know: the clearing was choked with brush and weeds, hiding a three-foot ledge of rock directly in front of my landing spot. The ledge slammed into the undercarriage as I hit. The plane snapped like a popper on the end of a bull whip. I was catapulted into a long head-first dive, like a man shot from a circus cannon. Fortunately, I landed in the brush and rolled to a stop in a sitting position. The padded leather ring that rimmed the cockpit hung from my neck like a lei. I was still holding the rubber grip pulled loose from the control stick. My seat belt lay across my lap. I felt around to determine that I had no broken bones. The wreckage of the plane was piled in a heap, like crumpled wastepaper.

Except for this lone field, the place appeared to be a wilderness of trees. After some exploration I located a little-used path and started to follow it. It meandered along for about half a mile and turned onto a dirt road that I followed downhill for perhaps another mile before I came to a small cabin. Sitting on a bench before the cabin were an elderly man and a woman, barefooted and dressed in work clothes. They smiled and waved. My first impression was astonishment at how clean they were, their scrubbed faces glowing above the faded calico and denim. I told them about the accident and about my mail pouches, which would have to be taken to a railroad station. They assured me that the rural mail carrier would be along shortly with his horse and rig and would willingly help me. The couple were very solicitous. Almost apologetically the wife brought out a big bowl of tiny wild strawberries, a jug of clotted cream, and a loaf of fresh home-baked bread.

Sure enough, the mail carrier came along in due course, with a sturdy mare pulling an old-fashioned hack. The old man and the mail carrier helped me bring the mail sacks down to the road and load them in the hack. Luckily there were only three or four sacks, hardly a hundred pounds.

After my thanks and good-bys, we drove about ten miles to Pithole, a little town on the railroad, where the stationmaster accepted the mail shipment. I used my Post Office travel commission to get a train ticket to Cleveland. It was quite a trip, my first flight with the mail.

On arrival in Cleveland from the forced landing at Pithole, I was surprised to hear little comment about my accident. Engine failure, forced landings, and crack-ups were so common on the Air Mail that, so long as the pilot was not killed or seriously hurt, no one gave them another thought. Teams of mechanics, ready for repair and salvage operations, were constantly busy.

The pilots worked constantly to make [bad-weather flying] less hazardous. For example, we learned there were many instances when we could fly all the way from Cleveland to New York if we could but get on top of the cloud bank. But if we had to stay underneath we sometimes couldn't cross the mountains. Often, when there were broken or scattered clouds at Cleveland and good weather reported from New York, the mountain country would provide an ideal situation for over-the-top flight. At other times the cloud deck would be solid at Cleveland. On such occasions, when the bottom of the clouds was high enough to allow for fall-out in a spin, I would try to climb up through. Eventually I was able to climb for quite a while, sometimes through several thousand feet of clouds.

The method I used was this: I would get set squarely in the middle of my seat, lock my heels against the floor boards, and, holding the rudder immobile and as close to neutral as possible, grasp the control stick between the thumb and forefinger of each hand; with the wings level I would pull up into a gentle climb. With the air-speed indicator, I could maintain an even speed in climbing, making corrections with exceedingly gentle movements of the controls and paying no attention to direction or compass heading. The natural stability of the plane helped to keep it level; if I felt a blast of air more strongly on one cheek, I would know that the wing was down and the plane slipping to that side. The problem was the false illusion of the senses, which would insistently tell you, because you could see neither ground nor horizon, that the plane was in some attitude or turn quite different from the fact; in time, this traitorous report would become so strong and so confusing that you would respond. If you yielded, you would soon stall and spin, or find yourself in a spiral or dive. Once losing your control you would have to cut the power and put the plane in a deliberate spin, so that you could come out of the clouds in a known condition, ready for a quick recovery.

Over-the-top flying had its charms. You were there in a peaceful world, alone. The only trouble was finding your way. On the deck, even though you'd be dodging steeples and scraping through winding passes, you always knew where you were. On top, however pleasant, there were no tracks to follow or landmarks. You knew the compass course but not the wind effect; the slower the airplane, the more potent the wind. Our early De Havillands cruised at around 85 or 90 miles an hour. Later, with improved propellers, windshields, and a modicum of streamlining, we got some of them up to 100. At such speeds a strong head wind can easily double a trip's normal time. A stiff side wind can make the plane crab along with a compass course as much as 45 degrees from normal. A calm-air trip from Newark to Cleveland would take a little over four hours. With a head wind it might take ten or eleven hours.

The one time I was in a bad enough fix to want to jump was in the days when we were still flying without parachutes. I believe that each surviving Air Mail pilot will tell you that at least once, early in his mail career, he had a brush with death that put the fear of God in him and made him acutely aware thenceforth that even the simplest error in judgment or a few seconds of carelessness might put his life in forfeit. Once a man got past that point safely, his chance of becoming a true professional pilot was much enhanced. I know that my ordeal marked a change in the quality of my work: I became not so much a more cautious pilot, for timidity has its dangers too, but a more thoughtful, careful one.

I was flying east out of Omaha in rainy, dirty weather, trying to make my way through the rolling country beyond Council Bluffs. The clouds were scraping the tops of the low hills. By ducking down into the hollows between the hills it was possible to see a little ahead, but in pulling over the higher rolls the fog would thicken and the ground dim, even with my wheels almost brushing the grass. I knew that in just a few miles I would reach a draw with a railroad in it that was two or three hundred feet lower than the terrain I was in, so I allowed myself to push on farther than I should have. As I went over one of the low hills the ground faded completely from sight, but I quickly eased the plane down and made it into the next hollow, where I was able to see a little. The hill ahead came at me fast, and instead of turning I was teased into climbing its slope. Again the ground faded from sight, but this time for more than a few seconds. When I eased back down, feeling for the next little valley, I did not see the surface until

I banged into it. The wheels evidently hit on a smooth grass field, for the plane, instead of crashing, bounced. Instinctively I pulled back on the stick, the plane shot up into the fog, and when it leveled off at several hundred feet I was completely in the soup.

While I still had a sense of orientation I tried to make a blind turn, and then leveled off again in what I hoped was the direction back. I turned, but a turn causes the compass to spin and swing; it takes some time before it can give a course indication. I now had no choice but to attempt to fly blind, locking the rudder in neutral, holding the stick in my finger-tips, feeling the wind on my cheeks, and watching the air-speed indicator. In this manner I was able to get the plane under some control and ease it down little by little, until my altimeter read that I was as low as I had been before. But I was unable to see anything of the ground, and the fog pouring back through my wings remained as thick and opaque as wet cotton. I dared not let down any lower or I would be bound to fly into the side of a hill, so I started to climb, mostly in desperation, for there was only a forlorn chance I could ever get on top of this type of weather.

Now followed a long period of fighting to keep control of the plane while all the time my equilibrium became steadily more confused. I succeeded in climbing to 8000 feet; then the plane began to get more and more out of control. It lost altitude until I was back down to 5000 feet. By this time I felt I had been milling around in the clouds for an eternity, and found myself wondering why I did not run out of fuel. At last I fell. The plane stalled and whipped off into a spin, although to my bewildered senses it did not seem to be spinning down, but impossibly up and to the side. I cut the throttle and held the plane in the spin for a few seconds to be certain I was in a known condition and to force my mind to reorient. When I broke the spin, I couldn't pull out level from the resulting dive. By the time I got the wires to stop screaming the plane promptly stalled again. The plane floundered through the dark muck in a series of stalls, spins, dives, and pull-outs. I struggled and fought with it all the way down, working with desperate concentration, but that little corner of my mind that detachedly views such things said, "My friend, you are a dead duck."

The altimeter needle was dropping fast and I knew I was low as I tried to recover from the fifth or sixth stall and spin. If I'd been in a Jenny I would have let it spin in, but a crash in a full spin in a DH-4 was almost always fatal, so I continued trying to right the plane. The wires were screaming from what seemed a full dive and I was pulling back hard to get the nose up when the tops of trees came flashing by, just below my wings. I was almost level. I rammed the stick forward to hold the plane there, cut both ignition switches, and coasted ahead, expecting to hit but not knowing what. The plane slid out under the deck of cloud to show me I was only 50 feet high —and over cleared land. We rolled to a stop, the propeller dead. After some minutes I began to tremble. I climbed out of the plane and had taken but two steps when my legs gave way.

On one trip, as I neared Chicago the quilted floor of fields and roads was marred by increasing patches of white fog, lying innocently here and there in shallow pools. There was enough visible ground to find my way until I was within a mile of the field, but then all was covered and the fog stretched solid to the east. The fog was fairly shallow, for I saw the mark of smoke, puddled in the white, from the tall smokestack that sat just west of the flying field. Circling over, I could just make out the circle of the stack's tip. Using it as a marker, I could line up with the runway, but when I glided down I could not even see the tips of my wings, and I had to push open the throttle and pull back on top. Circling, I saw that my propeller wash had made a gouge in the top of the fog as the plane dipped in, like a scoop taking ice cream from the top of a can. This gave me an idea: perhaps I could dig out enough fog to see the end of the runway.

It took a long time. I would dip in, then hold the plane's nose up in a near stall and jazz the engine to send the wash burning behind at a downward angle. After nearly an hour of circling and dipping I had dug out a ragged trough about 300 feet deep and could just see the end of the runway at its bottom. Touching down took care, for I had to start the glide beyond the edge of the hole, be blind for a moment, then have a few seconds to set the plane on the runway before I was blind in the fog again. A DH does not roll far on landing, the Maywood runway was broad and long, and the landing came off just fine. But the fog was so dense I could not see to taxi; men had to come out and guide me to the hangar.

To those on the ground my many circles and dips had sounded as though I was lost in the fog and desperately trying to dive into the field, although no one could understand how I could keep flying in the horrible muck. In the hangar, held from taking off by the fog, were the Army round-the-world fliers and their planes, just completed circling the globe and about to start a welcoming tour. They were, I believe, deeply impressed by the weather they saw the Air Mail come through. I did not explain how I had dug my way in.

6. Frank Hawks on Refueling an Airplane in Midair

When the late Emory Rogers opened an airport on Wilshire Boulevard and Fairfax Road—a section [of Los Angeles] now completely built up—I went with him as chief pilot at the munificent figure of $50 a week.

Just the other day I was reminded that at Rogers Airport in those days I gave her first airplane ride to Amelia Earhart. She told me that after being up with me for that first flight she decided she had to learn to fly herself, and within the year she had her pilot's license.

About July 1921 things were pretty dull around the airport. So I made a deal with Emory Rogers whereby I was to take one of his Standards and go out on barnstorming trips of a week or so duration in various localities that had thus far been more or less overlooked by enterprising airmen. Business was slow coming to us, so we adopted an old principle of economics and went out after the business. The net returns from these expeditions Rogers and I split fifty-fifty.

I worked along with satisfactory results for both of us until September 15 when I ran across a chap who had bought a Hispano-Suiza-motored Standard, considerably more powerful than the OX-5 jobs I had been flying. He was looking for a pilot to go out barnstorming with it on the usual basis of profit splitting. As I had only a roaming commission with Rogers and this looked like a better opportunity to make money, owing to the greater passenger capacity of the Hisso Standard, I jumped at the chance and was soon out on the road again leading the gypsy life of the barnstorming pilot.

Earl Dougherty had now established a little field of his own at Long Beach and was struggling along trying to make a go

Frank Hawks. (*The Bettmann Archive, Inc.*)

of it. His place was as much of a base as I had anywhere and both of us were always figuring up new stunts to attract the crowds, for crowds inevitably meant business in the form of passenger hops.

Mere acrobatic flying had come to be something of a drug on the aeronautical market and, to revive the public's flagging interest, I had tied up with a chap named Wesley May, a wing-walker and parachute-jumper. He and I would put on our act, which included straight and fancy wing walking, loops with May standing on the top wing, and sometimes even a transfer by Wesley from my ship to Dougherty's. Then May would do his parachute jump and I would proceed to capitalize on the free performance by landing and starting to take up the cash customers.

Even this was beginning to drag with the crowds, so Dougherty, May, and I got our heads together in an effort to figure out something new. The scheme that we evolved was to make aviation history, though none of us had that in mind. Briefly, it was to refuel one aircraft in flight from another and we advertised our coming stunt far and wide as a new "thriller" in the profession of thrills.

"That'll bring 'em out," Dougherty declared, "and then we'll clean up on passenger hops."

When the time came to carry out this hazardous and daring plan, a five-gallon can of gasoline was strapped on Wesley's back and I took off with him crouched on the top wing of my Standard.

Dougherty already was up in his Jenny and after maneuvering long enough to build up the right amount of suspense among those watching—or rather to give our "barker" on the ground a chance to build it up—we flew alongside the other ship.

May stood up and Dougherty jockeyed his Jenny in until his lower wing was overlapping our upper one. Then the daring wing-walker, who would have been courting death under any circumstances during such a mid-air transfer from plane to plane without a parachute but was doubly handicapped now with his awkward burden of fuel, reached up and grabbed the wing-skid of Dougherty's ship, lifting himself calmly onto the other plane as I dropped down to give them leeway.

Then, in full sight of the crowd and to the accompaniment of mad cheering which none of us could hear, he walked down the length of the wing to the fuselage and poured his can of gasoline into the Jenny's regular gas tank. The first successful refueling flight in the world had been completed!

7. Slats Rodgers on Flying Circus Acts

I kept thinking of flying. And I knew I'd fly someday, even if I had to build my own airplane. That's what I finally did.

I decided I was going to build a model plane. So I scared the chickens out of the henhouse and cleaned it out and got it ready to use as a workshop.

I began buying tools with whatever money I could spare. I made drawings of a model and started buying stuff to build it with. Building it wasn't easy at all. Most people then didn't even know what the devil airplanes were built out of.

I spent a lot of time in libraries reading all the stuff I could find about airplanes. Some of it was written by the Wright brothers. And I worked steady on my model plane until I finally had it finished, in about four months.

An airplane back in those days, in 1911, was just about as exciting to people as a flying saucer today—and to most of them it seemed just as cockeyed. "That thing won't ever fly," they all said, talking about airplanes.

One day a man came and introduced himself to me and told me he was with the magazine put out for the men who worked on the railroad, the Santa Fe.

"That little plane of yours sure is causing a lot of talk," he said. "I'd like to talk to you and get a picture of it to put in the magazine."

I said, fine.

"What's the idea of building it?" he asked me.

"I'm going to build a real one that I can fly in," I said.

"Well, more power to you," he said, and grinned.

About that time a woman opened a picture show there in Cleburne. Picture shows were about as strange and new as airplanes. The woman offered me 75 bucks to put my model airplane in front of her show for a week, and I told her it was a deal. That gave me a start toward my real plane.

I took my plans to a draftsman, Steve Haywood, a Santa Fe man, and he got steamed up about it and helped me all he could. I needed help because my plans weren't accurate at all.

Lots of people began hurrahing me about the plane. "Flying is for birds," they said. "Those things won't ever work."

I didn't pay them any mind, but kept on getting all the dope I could find on how to build a plane, such things as the right wing curve and the size of wings and all that. I finally figured out that a 30-foot wingspread would be about right.

I started ordering materials and getting ready to do the building. I ordered spruce from Oregon. There were no turnbuckles like I needed in this country, so I had to order those from France.

I bought the engine in St. Louis for $750. It was a 6-cylinder engine, weighing 287 pounds, and was rated at 100 horsepower.

There weren't any other airplanes being built in Texas

then. Mine was the first. So everybody was mighty curious.

The last job was to get the linen to cover it with. In those days there was none of that dope you use to tighten cloth on wings, and nobody knew how to make it. Back to the library I went and found out that a mixture of celluloid, acetone, ether, and banana oil would do the job.

I didn't know anything about chemistry, but it seemed to me that stuff might blow up if you put it all together. It didn't blow up, but it worked so good it tightened the cloth too much and warped the wings almost in a circle. We had to cut the cloth and put in patches. Finally we got it finished and set it up outside.

I put a big tent wall up around the ship so nobody could gawk at it free, then advertised that I would show it on a certain day at 50 cents a throw. The day came and so did the people. I never knew there were so many people. After showing for three days I had $700 in cash.

"When you gonna fly it?" everybody kept asking me.

Some others asked different questions and said things like "It's built wrong," and "A man can't teach hisself to fly," and "Nobody but a crazy man would get in that."

What I wanted was a big, smooth field to put the ship on so I could get set to fly. About three miles north of town a man named Hill had a pasture that was plenty big and pretty level. I went to him and asked him how about using it.

"Sure, Slats," he said. "Use it as long as you want to. But if you keep fooling with that trap you won't be needing it very long."

That was late in 1912, the year a lot of men who figured big in the story of flying were building jackknife crates just about like mine and flying them—or trying to fly them.

I finally got my ship out to the pasture. A big crowd followed me all the way, even though it was pitch dark. When I got to the pasture the people stood around waiting for me to do something.

As soon as it was daylight I cranked the motor and started trying to taxi down the field. It was like driving a blind hog to water. It wouldn't go any place I wanted it to.

I fooled with the ship for a while then decided I couldn't make much headway right at first, so I stretched some ropes around it, put a watchman on, and went home.

I couldn't keep the crowd away. They swarmed out there every day, watching everything I did, telling me how to fly it and why it wouldn't fly. And laughing all the time like hyenas. I wasn't getting anywhere trying to fly, not even on the ground.

If I got up much speed she'd ground loop and smash the wire wheels and maybe bust a wing tip. I spent about half my time patching the ship, the other half busting it up again moving around on the ground.

For aileron control I had a little yoke made out of tubing covered with wool. It fit around my shoulders. I snapped the aileron wires to this yoke. If the right wing got down, I would lean to the left, and if the left wing got down, I would lean to the right.

Finally I began to learn a little about what the rudder was for and how to work the rest of the controls all at the same time. I got so I could run in something pretty close to a straight line.

I guess it was a good thing I spent all that time grass-cutting instead of trying to fly right away. I began to get the feel of the ship. I think the reason I never got excited in later years when I was coming in for a crash was all that time I spent flying on the ground.

Slats Rodgers at the controls of *Old Soggy No. 1*. (*Rapp Collection*)

I'd been doing all my flying that way for about six weeks when one day I got shed of the ground for the first time, and not because I intended to. I had to. I got her going down the field and all of a sudden I noticed a ditch right in front of me. I hadn't seen it before, but there it was. I knew I had to jump the ditch or crack up good. I pulled back on the wheel and she jumped about 30 feet in the air. She kept going in the air for 200 feet or so.

That was my first flight. It ended just like a lot of other flights later on, in a crack-up. The ship came down hard, and the right wing hit first. It dragged along the ground and broke off. Then the plane swung around, and all three wheels broke.

I didn't get hurt. I walked away.

Here came the crowd yelling, "She flew! I saw it fly!"

Same old thing, one day after another. I couldn't fly. Couldn't control the thing. The right wing always came down and banged into the ground. It just wasn't made exactly right.

"I'm gonna fly her or tear her apart," I said.

In the center of the field there was a little knoll. It was smooth—just a sort of rise. I ran at it full speed. When I hit it the plane bounced about 40 feet in the air. The right wing went down the way it always did. That wing was just plain soggy—that's why I called her *Old Soggy No. 1.*

I leaned to the left hard. The wing came up. That was the first time I ever got that wing up—first time I'd ever been in the air long enough to work on it.

I hit the ground and rolled along in fine shape, with all three wheels working, something else brand new for me. So I taxied back to where the boys were and got them to help me fill her with gas.

"I'm gonna light out of here," I said. "This time I'm not going to cut the motor."

Off I went. I hit the knoll and the ship bounced in the air just fine—and the right wing went down. I yanked it back up O.K. and kept it up. I had to fly leaning to the left all the time, but I was flying—I knew that when I looked down and saw a house passing under me. I was *really* flying that time. I'd left my little field behind.

What did the Wright brothers have on me? Well, for one thing they knew how to turn a ship in the air and I didn't. I started to turn the thing and I felt it slipping and quivering so I straightened it back up in a hurry. I never had seen anybody fly a ship—I never had even seen one except mine. And I hadn't got around to reading that part in the book that told how to bank when you turn or you slip right on off.

I could see a big cornfield in front of me, and I made for

it because I could get there without turning. I set her down in the corn patch and didn't crack her up.

I first landed at Love Field early in 1919. I got to liking the place, so I landed there whenever I flew that way, and sometimes I spent the night in Dallas. Pretty soon a few of us, mainly Clint Foster and me at first, got to hauling passengers.

When passengers didn't show up fast enough, why, we'd do a little stunting to get a crowd. Most of the stunt fliers were young fellows, men just out of war. I was around thirty then, and they considered me an old man. A lot of the young pilots were better at stunting than I was, and some of them began getting better ships.

But I pretty much held my own with them. I figured what the crowd loved was noise and low flying. That's what I gave them. By that time I had learned to come down onto the field, touch the ground with the wheels, and go for a loop, a stunt that not many other fliers tried then, one reason being that they couldn't in a Jenny or Canuck. I did it in a Travelair that I got hold of, and I did a lot of checking first up high, to be sure I didn't lose any altitude in making the loop. Then, when I was pretty sure, why I came down, kissed the ground, and went for one. It worked, even if I did get gravel in my face sometimes from my own prop wash.

It was hard for me to believe that a man like me was called Pop way back there in the days when flying was brand new and when people would drive half a day just to see a ship take off —or just to see it on the ground. There were millions of people back in 1920 who had never seen an airplane, and millions of others who were dead certain the things wouldn't really fly.

The air shows we put on in those days weren't all alike. We kept trying to think up new stunts.

Barnstormer Slats Rodgers. (*Rapp Collection*)

The pants race always gave the crowd a kick. They would line up four or five ships side by side, and close to each ship they would mark a circle, about eight feet in diameter, with lime. Then, when the pilots got their motors going, the flag man would give them the signal and off they would go. They didn't go far, for the idea was to get back to that circle as fast as you could once you were in the air.

When you got back, you had to jump out of the ship, take off your pants, leave them inside the circle, then get back in the ship and take off again. Then back you came and jumped out and put your pants back on.

Zippers sure would have helped in those races. But most of us were smart enough not to have anything buttoned when we started.

The winner of the race would get maybe 75 bucks.

I did pretty good in the pants races, mainly because I could get out of the ship and get my pants off and get back in the ship so fast.

I think the best air show we ever staged was at Wichita Falls back around 1923. The people at Wichita were expecting plenty, for they'd heard a lot about the Lunatics of Love Field, and all the Dallas crowd was going up. The big secret was that I was going to throw out a dummy. Nobody knew that except one ambulance driver who was to beat all the other ambulance drivers to the dummy when it hit, and a couple of fellows helping rig things for the stunt.

We got a man in Dallas to make up the dummy, and he did a fine job. That dummy was good-looking. Once in a while I'd catch myself talking to the thing. He had on polished boots and wore a helmet and goggles—all decked out.

Well, when the time came to take off for Wichita, I was ready and thought I had a freshly rebuilt ship with plenty of power and in good shape. An old man was standing there watching me get ready, and he said, "I'd like to ride up there with you if nobody else is going along. I've never had a ride in an airplane and I want to see the air show."

I stopped tinkering with the plane and looked at him.

"You know what you're saying?" I asked him.

"Sure."

"All right. Be ready pretty soon. I'll be shoving off in half an hour."

Along came Major Bill Long, a friend of mine who was in the airplane business at Love Field, and said, "Slats, I've got something to help out with the show."

"Let's have it," I said.

"I've got a wind-driven siren. Let's put it on your landing gear and give them some noise up there."

They fastened that siren on and put on a brake so I could start and stop it from the cockpit.

I yelled at the helper to turn the prop a couple of times to load her with gas. "Switch is off," I said.

That's what I thought. When he gave that prop a twist the motor started. Dangerous business—men have got their heads sliced in half that way. I called the mechanic out and told him the ignition switch wouldn't cut off. He said he was taking off for Wichita himself, and he'd fix it up there.

To cut off the gas supply from the carburetor I had to get out on the ground, take a pair of pliers, and turn the valve. Couldn't cut it off from the cockpit. But what the h——.

It was a pretty day for flying, and when we got somewhere around Bowie I decided it was too quiet, so I turned on the siren. Sure made a big racket. Me and the [old] man were half deaf in no time at all, so I decided to cut the thing off. I squeezed the handle put on there to cut it off. It kept going. I couldn't cut the thing off at all. The brake contraption they rigged wouldn't work.

On we went, raising the dead for miles around.

A little farther along I saw that the motor was turning too fast. I pulled back on the throttle. Nothing happened that time, either. I pulled all the way back. No good. The piano wire had broken in the conduit.

There I was, siren wide open, throttle wide open, engine roaring, about to fly apart any minute, and I couldn't cut off anything. I knew that motor might never hold together—I kept expecting to see connecting rods and pistons go flying all over the place.

There was only one thing to do—go on in and fly over the field until I ran out of gas.

She held together for an hour and ten minutes while I circled the field, siren going all the time, everybody in the country coming to see what was wrong. When she finally popped out of gas I started down.

Just as the wheels touched the ground and I set the tail end down for a landing, more gas ran into the carburetor and the motor roared again, wide open. Off we went, siren screaming, motor roaring, people on the ground scattering.

I knew she wouldn't run far, so I made a tight turn. When I got about halfway around she popped out of gas again.

I headed her back in and as soon as she hit the ground I jumped out and grabbed the left wing. More gas seeped into the carburetor and the motor began running fast again. I hung on. Round and round we went, me digging up dirt with my heels, the motor roaring, the [old] man trying to get out. I yelled to stay where he was, but he'd had enough of that business. He wanted to feel the ground under his feet.

The men around the field were afraid to come out. They didn't know which way the ship was going next. When they finally did get to the ship I was all out of breath, but I was still hanging on and the motor was just sputtering.

"What's the matter?" some monkey asked.

"You think of something that ain't the matter," I said.

Around 2:30 in the afternoon we got the show going. I was to fly Gene Brewer, the trick man, on the wings. The crowds that always showed up for that stunt just knew someday I'd throw Gene off and he'd bust wide open like a watermelon when he hit the ground. He didn't wear a parachute—so if he ever let go that was it.

Well, that time we rigged it so we could give the crowd what it wanted. We were going to bust Gene Brewer wide open for them. I took Gene up and he went all over the wings

A wing-walker in action. (*U.S. Air Force*)

and back to the tail section—gave the crowd a big thrill, and he gave me a thrill, too. The way that man could crawl around on a ship made the skin on your back crawl.

That was just a preview, though.

The main event was to take place later, around 5:30. I was to take Brewer up again, and he was to climb out of the cockpit onto the wings while I was looping. That's when we were going to flash the dummy on them.

We had put the dummy in the turtleback of Slim Madison's car. Slim was one of the boys who helped me with the show.

I got in the ship, strapped myself in, and told Slim to give me the dummy. I hauled it in and put it in my lap. With that dummy in the cockpit I could barely move the stick, but I shoved off. The crowd wanted a show—I'd give them one.

I got up to about 1500 feet, went for a loop, and at the top of the loop, when I was upside down, I let the dummy go off on his own. Worked just fine. He went twisting and whirling down and fell right in the center of the field.

Our ambulance man who was on the inside had a good start by the time the dummy was on the way down, and he got to the dummy about the time the other ambulances got started.

There were around 16,000 people out for that show, and the whole mob of them started swarming toward the spot where the dummy hit. But before they could get there our ambulance man had the dummy in his car and was headed for the Elm Street Hospital. The cops were clearing the way. They sure were nice to that dummy—had their sirens wide open rushing him to a doctor.

When they got to the hospital and opened the door and dragged out the dummy, one of the cops slammed his cap down on the ground and jumped on it.

We had done almost everything else back in those early days, so we decided to have a night air circus at Love Field. We had it. Like to have been the end of it for me. I flew the ship with the fireworks in it.

My ship was wired so that all I had to do was push the button and all the fuses started fusing and the fireworks started firing. The fireworks were on the wings. They'd have burned the ship down to the motor in a hurry if it had been standing still, but we figured with the ship moving the wind would pull the fire away from the wings.

I hoped it would work that way, since I was the one who was going to be in the ship.

I was 3000 feet high and flying from the back cockpit. I pushed the button and all at once the fireworks lit up and I was blind as a bat, a lot of sizzling and fizzing right in my face. I held her level as long as I could, which wasn't very long. I lost control and she went spinning to the right. When I pulled her out of that, she went spinning to the left.

That time I was sure I would spin in. But I didn't get excited. Same old story—I kept trying to do the best I could. But I was losing altitude fast, even though I didn't know exactly how fast because I couldn't see the instrument board.

Finally all those fireworks burned out, and after wallowing around up there a while longer I got so I could see again. I saw the lights of Dallas, then I flew around for a little and found Love Field and came on in. The crowd was the biggest that had ever come out to the field, and the people whooped it up when I landed, honking their automobile horns and yelling their heads off.

"Finest acrobatics we've ever seen," one guy says to me.

The show was to go on for another night, and I was to go up again and burn some brand-new fireworks. But that time I rigged for it. I went to a tin shop and had them make me a long horn, one about ten inches in diameter and reaching from the rear cockpit up close to the engine. Then, when I set off the fireworks, I had a hole to look through.

I got lined up beforehand on the lights of Dallas and I never let go of those lights until the fizzing and popping and shining on the wings stopped. Nothing to it. But the crowd didn't like that show near as much as the first.

8. Richard Evelyn Byrd
on Flying to the North Pole

There were two fairly good reasons for our wanting to fly to the North Pole: first, by traveling at high altitude over unexplored regions we might discover some new land or unexpected scientific phenomena; second, a successful flight would be sure to accelerate public interest in aviation.

[Floyd Bennett and I] selected for our flight a Fokker three-engine monoplane. One was available that had already flown 20,000 miles. It had 200-horsepower Wright air-cooled motors, any two of which would keep it up for a certain reduced distance.

We arrived at Kings Bay, Spitzbergen [Norway], at 4 P.M. April 29 [1926]. We found that we had to dig down through the snow and build a fire and put the cans of oil in the fire before we could pour it into the engines, which had already been heated by a big fireproof canvas bag covering them leading by a funnel down to a gasoline stove below.

Byrd's plane, the *Josephine Ford,* a Fokker tri-motor. (*U.S. Air Force*)

As there was no level stretch available that was smooth enough to take off from with a heavy load, we were forced to try another new stunt—to take off going down hill. The plane's first attempt to take off for a trial flight ended in a snowdrift. A ski was broken to bits and the landing gear bent and broken. Then twice again we broke our ski in pretty much the same way.

Final preparations were completed on May 8. We warmed the motors; heated our fuel oil; put the last bit of fuel and food aboard; examined our instruments with care. Bennett and I climbed in and we were off.

Off, but alas, not up. Our load proved too great, the snow too "bumpy," the friction of the skis too strong a drag. The plane simply would not get into the air. We got off the end of the runway at a terrific speed, jolted roughly over snow hummocks, and landed in a snowdrift.

We dug out of the snowdrift and concluded to work through the night lengthening and smoothing the runway. At the same time we would take out of the plane as much equipment as we could spare, and attempt a takeoff with a little less fuel. We decided to try to get off as near midnight as possible, when the night cold would make the snow harder and therefore easier to take off from.

Bennett and I had had almost no sleep for 36 hours, but that did not bother us. We decided to give full power and full speed—and get off or crash at the end of the runway in the jagged ice.

With a total load of nearly 10,000 pounds we raced down the runway. The rough snow ahead loomed dangerously near but we never reached it. We were off for our great adventure!

We looked ahead at the sea ice gleaming in the rays of the midnight sun—a fascinating scene whose lure had drawn famous men into its clutches, never to return. It was with a feeling of exhilaration that we felt that for the first time in history two mites of men could gaze upon its charms, and discover its secrets, out of reach of those sharp claws.

Perhaps! There was still that "perhaps," for if we should have a forced landing disaster might easily follow.

Our chief concern was to steer as nearly due north as possible. This could not be done with the ordinarily dependable magnetic compass, which points only in the general direction of the North Magnetic Pole, lying on Boothia Peninsula, Canada, more than a thousand miles south of the North Geographical Pole.

There was only one thing to do—to depend upon the sun. For this we used a sun-compass.

With the sun-compass, the time of day is known, and the shadow of the sun, when it bisects the head of the 24-hour clock, indicates the direction.

Then there was the influence of the wind that had to be allowed for. If, for example, a 30-mile-an-hour wind is blowing at right angles to the course, the plane will be taken 30 miles an hour to one side of its course. This is called "drift" and can be compensated for by an instrument called the drift-indicator [which we used] through the trapdoor in the plane.

I froze my face and one of my hands in taking sights with the instruments from the trapdoors. But I noticed these frost-bites at once and was more careful thereafter.

We were flying at about 2000 feet, and I could see at least 50 miles in every direction. There was no sign of land. If there had been any within 100 miles' radius we would have seen its mountain peaks, so good was the visibility.

Richard Evelyn Byrd in 1925. (*National Archives*)

When our calculations showed us to be about an hour from the Pole, I noticed through the cabin window a bad leak in the oil tank of the starboard motor. Bennett confirmed my fears. He wrote: "That motor will stop."

Bennett then suggested that we try landing to fix the leak. But I had seen too many expeditions fail by landing. We decided to keep on for the Pole. We would be in no worse fix should we come down near the Pole than we would be if we had a forced landing where we were.

At 9:02 A.M., May 9, 1926, Greenwich civil time, our calculations showed us to be at the Pole! The dream of a lifetime had at last been realized.

We headed to the right to take two confirming sights of the sun, then turned and took two more. After that we went on for several miles in the direction we had come, and made another larger circle to be sure to take in the Pole. We thus made a nonstop flight around the world in a very few minutes.

Below us was a great eternally frozen, snow-covered ocean, broken into ice fields or cakes of various sizes and shapes, the boundaries of which were the ridges formed by the great pressure of one cake upon another. This showed a constant ice movement and indicated the non-proximity of land.

At 9:15 A.M. we headed for Spitzbergen. The reaction of having accomplished our mission, together with the narcotic effect of the motors, made us drowsy. I dozed off once at the wheel and had to relieve Bennett several times because of his sleepiness.

We were aiming for Grey Point, Spitzbergen, and finally when we saw it dead ahead, we knew that we had been able to keep on our course! That motor was still running. We afterward found out the leak was caused by a rivet jarring out of its hole, and when the oil got down to the level of the hole it stopped leaking.

It seemed but a few moments until we were in the arms of our comrades, who carried us with wild joy down the snow runway.

9. Charles A. Lindbergh on Flying Solo Nonstop from New York to Paris

Why shouldn't I fly from New York to Paris? I'm almost twenty-five. I have more than four years of aviation behind me, and close to two thousand hours in the air. I've barnstormed over half of the 48 states. I've flown my mail through the worst of nights.

*

I'm talking to Harry Knight in his brokerage office at Fourth and Olive Streets [St. Louis]. "If we can get the plane and engine manufacturers to stand part of the expense, I think ten thousand dollars would be enough," I tell him. "If we can't get them to take part, it might cost as much as fifteen thousand to buy the plane and engine, and make the flight."

Knight suddenly swings around in his chair, and picks up the telephone. "Get me Harold Bixby at the State National Bank," he says . . . "Bix, how about coming over here for a few minutes?"

Within ten minutes Bixby knocks on the door. He's a man you like right away—smiling and full of humor. Harry Knight outlines my project for flying an airplane from St. Louis to New York to Paris.

"You think a plane with a Whirlwind engine can make a flight like that?" Bixby asks.

"Yes, sir," I answer.

"Slim, don't you think you ought to have a plane with more than one engine for that kind of flight?" Bixby asks.

Harry Knight laughs. "That's what I asked him, Bix; but he doesn't think it would be much safer."

"Suppose one of the engines cuts out halfway across the ocean," I put in. "I couldn't get to shore with the other two . . . A pilot can't fly at all without taking *some* risk. I've weighed my chances pretty carefully . . ."

*

"Do you mind waiting? Mr. Bixby is still in conference. He'll be through in just a few minutes."

The secretary smiles and leaves. It's ten o'clock. I sit down in a corner chair at the State National Bank of St. Louis.

I shift in my chair. My clothes bind; my collar sticks around my neck. I feel out of place. Mine is not a business proposition. How can a bank afford to back a flight across the ocean? I want to take off a heavily overloaded airplane with one engine, fly through unknown weather, over thousands of miles of land and water where a single crack in an oil line would mean a crash. I want to—

"Hello Slim! I'm sorry I had to keep you waiting. I've been jammed up this morning."

Bixby slips in through one of those waist-high mahogany semiprivate gates. I stand to shake hands.

"Slim, you've sold us on this proposition of yours," he says.

69

"It's a tough job you're taking on, but we've talked it over and we're with you. From now on you'd better leave the financial end to us."

*

The Ryan Airlines factory is an old, dilapidated building near the [San Diego] waterfront. There's no flying field, no hangar, no sound of engines warming up.

"If we place our order with your company," [I ask] "will you guarantee to give us a plane with range enough to fly from New York to Paris?"

[Company president B. F.] Mahoney shifts his weight uncomfortably on the table. "I don't see how we can do that," he says. "The risks are too high . . . We'll do the best we can. But at six thousand dollars we can't go overboard on guarantees."

I'm ready to cast my lot with the Ryan organization. I believe in [engineer Donald] Hall's ability; I like Mahoney's enthusiasm. I have confidence in the character of the workmen I've met. This company is a fit partner for our organization in St. Louis. They're as anxious to build a plane that will fly to Paris as I am to fly it there.

*

Donald Hall and I sit down on the long curving beach at Coronado Strand. It's pleasantly warm in the morning sun.

"Where are we going to put the cockpit?"

"I'd like to have it behind the gas tank—about where it is in the [Ryan airplane model] M-2," I reply.

"But then you couldn't see straight ahead," he argues. "The tanks would be directly in front of you. I thought you would want to sit behind the engine so as to have the best possible vision."

"You know we always look out at an angle when we take

off," I tell him. "The nose of the fuselage blocks out the field straight ahead, anyway . . . I don't need straight forward vision . . ."

"I'm not referring to takeoff," Hall says . . . "I'm thinking of forward vision in normal flight."

"There's not much need to see ahead in normal flight," I reply. "When I'm near a flying field, I can watch the sky ahead by making shallow banks. Why don't we leave the cockpit in the rear. All I need is a window on each side to see out through. I don't like the idea of being sandwiched in between the engine and a gas tank the way you are up forward. If you crack up you haven't got a chance in a place like that. A compass won't work as well, either, close to the engine. I've got to have an accurate compass on this flight."

"All right. The cockpit goes in the rear, then," Hall says . . . "O.K. Now what night-flying equipment do you want to put in the plane?"

"None. Those things are nice to have, but we can't afford the weight."

"How about a parachute?"

"Same answer," I reply. "That would cost almost twenty pounds."

Hall makes some notes on his pad. "Well, if you don't have to carry those things, it will make it a lot easier for me," he says. "Say, I'm not satisfied with the size of the M-2 tail surfaces. They ought to be bigger for a heavy-load takeoff, and to get good stability in cruising flight."

"Wouldn't bigger surfaces cut down the range?"

"A little, but not very much."

"Let's put everything into range," I say. "I don't need a very stable plane. I'll have to be watching the compass all the time anyway. I don't plan on going to sleep while I fly."

The *Spirit of St. Louis.* (*U.S. Air Force*)

Thirty revolutions low! The engine's vibrating roar throbs back through the fuselage and drums heavily on taut fabric skin.

Thirty revolutions low—a soft runway, a tail wind, an over-load. I glance down at the wheels. They press deeply, tires bulging, into the wet, sandy clay.

My cockpit quivers with the engine's tenseness. Sharp explosions from the exhaust stacks speak with confidence and precision. But the *Spirit of St. Louis* isn't vibrant with power as it's always been before.

The mechanics, the engineers, the blue-uniformed police officers standing there behind the wing, everyone has done his part. Now, it's up to me.

Their eyes are intently on mine. They've seen planes crash before. They know what a wrong decision means. If I shake my head, there'll be no complaint, no criticism; I'll be welcomed back into their midst, back to earth and life.

Wind, weather, power, load—gradually these elements stop

churning in my mind. It's less a decision of logic than of feeling, the kind of feeling that comes when you gauge the distance to be jumped between two stones across a brook . . . Sitting in the cockpit, the conviction surges through me that the wheels *will* leave the ground, that the wings *will* rise above the wires, that it *is* time to start the flight.

I buckle my safety belt, pull goggles down over my eyes, turn to the men at the blocks, and nod . . . A yank on the ropes —the wheels are free. I brace myself against the left side of the cockpit, sight along the edge of the runway, and ease the throttle wide open.

But, except for noise and vibration, what little effect the throttle has! The plane creeps heavily forward. Several men are pushing on wing struts to help it start.

There's none of the spring forward that always before preceded the takeoff into air—no lightness of wing, no excess power. The stick wobbles loosely from side to side, and slipstream puts hardly any pressure against rudder. Nothing about my plane has the magic quality of flight. But men begin stumbling off from the wing struts. We're going faster.

Pace quickens—turf becomes a blur—the tail skid lifts off ground—

The halfway mark streaks past . . . seconds now to decide —close the throttle, or will I get off? The wrong decision means a crash—probably in flames—I pull the stick back firmly, and—*The wheels leave the ground* . . . The wheels touch again . . . Off again—right wing low—pull it up—Ease back onto the runway . . . The next hop's longer—I could probably stay in air; but I let the wheels touch once more—lightly.

The *Spirit of St. Louis* takes herself off the next time—full flying speed—the controls taut, alive, straining.

I bank cautiously northward until [the compass] rises to the center line—65 degrees—the compass heading for the first 100-mile segment of my great-circle route [from New York] to France and Paris. It's 7:54 [A.M.] Eastern daylight time [May 20, 1927].

Miles slip by quickly as I skim over the ocean farther from New York, closer to Paris; the haze clearing, the clouds lifting. Then, a fishing smack, appearing off my starboard wing, reminds me that I'm flying below mast-top level. I let the *Spirit of St. Louis* rise a few feet.

One o'clock; it's lunch time in New York.

Lunch time! I drop my hand to the bag of sandwiches, but I'm not hungry. Why eat simply because it's lunch time? A drink of water will be enough.

The sky has been filling slowly: first, a few stray cumulus clouds, blinding in the sunlight; then flocks of them. A solid mass blocks out the north—tremendous, dark, and foreboding. Angular streaks of gray break the horizon ahead into segments—rain squalls.

As I approach these storm clouds, air is really getting rough. Wing tips flex with rapid, jerking movements, and the cockpit bumps up, down, and sideways.

The wings were never designed for such a wrenching! I feel as though the storm were gathering my plane in its teeth as a dog picks up a rabbit. If only I had a parachute! But there's no use wishing for things I don't have.

The edge of the storm recedes gradually.

If I could throw myself down on a bed, I'd be asleep in an instant. In fact, if I didn't know the result, I'd fall asleep just as I am, sitting up in the cockpit—I'm beyond the stage where I need a bed, or even to lie down. This is only afternoon. If sleep weighs so heavily on me now, how can I get through the night, to say nothing of the dawn, and another day, and its

74

night, and possibly even the dawn after? Something must be done—immediately.

I pull the *Spirit of St. Louis* up two or three hundred feet above the water, shake my head and body roughly, flex muscles of my arms and legs, stamp my feet on the floor boards. The nose veers sharply left, and I have to put my toes back on the rudder to straighten it out. I breathe deeply, and squirm about as much as I can while still holding the controls.

*

The first quarter of my flight is behind. There's a sense of real accomplishment in that fact. How satisfying it is to have 800 miles behind—No! that's the wrong tack. Sleep has crept up a notch. Anything that's satisfying is relaxing. I can't afford to relax. I must think about *problems*—concentrate on difficulties ahead.

Suddenly I become aware of a white pyramid below me— an iceberg, lustrous white against the water. I've never seen anything so white before. It draws my eyes from the instruments and makes me conscious of a strange new sea. Ahead and on each side are several more. So that's why surface ships stay south in warmer waters! Well, I'm flying high enough to miss these drifting crags. Soon there are icebergs everywhere —white patches on a blackened sea; sentries of the Arctic.

*

I'm flying with my head thrown back, looking up through the skylight at the handful of stars above me, glancing down at intervals to make sure my compass heading is correct. Looking straight up for guidance is like dangling at the end of a rope; it's almost impossible to keep from turning slightly.

The stars blink on and off as haze thickens in places and then thins out again. I hold on to them tightly, dreading the blind flying that lies ahead the moment I let them go. Soon haze becomes so thick that, except for those dim points of light, it might as well be cloud. At any moment those stars may blink their last and die.

Why try to hold on to those stars? Why not start in now on instruments? The *Spirit of St. Louis* is too unstable to fly well on instruments. It's fast, and it has a greater range than any plane that flies; but it's high-strung, and balanced on a pin point. If I relax pressure on stick or rudder for an instant, the nose will veer off course.

And there's the question of staying awake. Could I keep sufficiently alert during long, monotonous hours of flying with my eyes glued to the instruments, with nothing more to stimulate my mind than the leaning of a needle?

A pillar of cloud blocks out the stars ahead, spilling over on top like a huge mushroom in the sky. I tighten my belt, push the nose down a bit, and adjust the stabilizer for level flight. In the seconds that intervene while I approach, I make the mental and physical preparation for blind flying.

Wings quiver as I enter the cloud. Air roughens until it jerks the *Spirit of St. Louis* about as though real demons were pulling at fuselage and wings. Everything is uniform blackness, except for the exhaust's flash on passing mist and the glowing dials in my cockpit.

Flying blind is difficult enough in smooth air. In this swirling cloud, it calls for all the concentration I can muster. The turn and bank indicators, the air speed, the altimeter, and the compass, all those phosphorescent lines and dots in front of me, must be kept in proper place. When a single one strays off, the rest go chasing after it like so many sheep and have to be caught quickly and carefully herded back into position again.

It's cold up here at—I glance at the altimeter—10,500 feet

—*cold*—good Lord, there *are* things to be considered outside the cockpit! How could I forget! I jerk off a leather mitten and thrust my arm out the window. My palm is covered with stinging pinpricks. I pull the flashlight from my pocket and throw its beam onto a strut. The entering edge is irregular and shiny—ice!

I've got to turn around, get back into clear air—quickly!

Charles A. Lindbergh. (*The Bettmann Archive, Inc.*)

My eyes sense a change in the blackness of my cockpit. I look out through the window. Can those be the same stars? Is this the same sky? How bright! How clear! What safety I have reached! I was in the thunderhead for ten minutes at most; but it's one of those incidents that can't be measured by minutes.

I turn southward, skirting the edge of the cloud pillar. I'll have to fly around these thunderheads. But can I? For the first time, the thought of turning back seriously enters my mind. I can climb another five or six thousand feet. The [cloud] canyons up there may be wider. If they're not, and I can find no passes [through the storm] east or southward, I'll have to turn back . . . for another start from that narrow, muddy runway on Long Island.

The pillars of cloud multiply and thicken. I follow narrow canyons between them, weaving in and out around thunderheads, taking always the southward choice for course.

Fourteen hundred miles behind. Twenty-two hundred miles to go. All readings normal. I throw my flashlight onto the wing strut again. The coating of ice is thinner. It's evaporating slowly. The haze continues to clear.

Lights! There are lights under my left wing. A ship on the ocean!

What's the matter?—The lights are rising—They're too far apart for lights on a ship ten thousand feet below—They're gone all together—flashed off as they flashed on! I turn to the instruments; yes, I've been flying right wing low. I must have been looking at some stars.

I've lost command of my eyelids. When they start to close, I can't restrain them. They shut, and I shake myself, and lift them with my fingers.

I've *got* to find some way to keep alert. There's no alternative but death and failure. I try running fast on the floorboards with my feet for as many seconds as the *Spirit of St. Louis* will hold to course. Then, I clamp the stick between my knees while I simulate running with my hands.

I take off my helmet—rub my head—pull the helmet on again—I drink some water from the canteen—that helps. Possibly if I eat a sandwich. I've had nothing since breakfast yesterday; but my mouth wants no food, and eating might make me sleepier.

Shaking my body and stamping my feet no longer has effect. It's more fatiguing than arousing. I'll have to try something else. I push the stick forward and dive down into a high ridge of cloud, pulling up sharply after I clip through its summit. That wakes me a little, but tricks don't help for long. They're only tiring. It's better to sit still and conserve strength.

During long ages between dawn and sunrise, I'm thankful we didn't make the *Spirit of St. Louis* a stable plane. The very instability which makes it difficult to fly blind or hold an accurate course at night now guards me against excessive errors. Its veering prods my lagging senses. The slightest relaxation of pressure on either stick or rudder starts a climbing or a diving turn, hauling me back from the borderland of sleep.

The waves ahead disappear. Fog covers the sea.

The fog doesn't pass. I go on and on through its white blankness. I'm growing accustomed to blind flying. I've done almost as much on this single trip as on all my flights before put together.

I'm twenty-one hours from New York.

Will the fog never end?

While I'm staring at the instruments the fuselage behind me becomes filled with ghostly presences—vaguely outlined forms, transparent, moving, riding weightless with me in the plane. These phantoms speak with human voices—friendly,

79

vaporlike shapes, without substance, able to vanish or appear at will, to pass in and out through the walls of the fuselage as though no walls were there.

Mist lightens—the *Spirit of St. Louis* bursts into brilliant sunlight, dazzling to fog-accustomed eyes—a blue sky—sparkling whitecaps. Brilliant light, opening sky, and clarity of waves fill me with hope. I've probably passed through the great body of the storm.

Sunbeams are moving in the cockpit. The nose is veering north. I push right rudder. I've been daydreaming; I must be more careful. The sunbeams are a great help. Their movements catch my eye more quickly than the compass needle or the turn indicator.

I'm flying along dreamily when it catches my eye, that black speck on the water two or three miles southeast. I squeeze my lids together and look again. A boat! A small boat! Several small boats, scattered over the surface of the ocean!

I dive down. There's no sign of life on deck. I fly over to the next boat. Its deck is empty too. But as I drop my wing to circle, a man's head appears, thrust out through a cabin porthole, motionless, staring up at me. I fly on eastward.

Is that a cloud on the northeastern horizon, or a strip of low fog—or—*can it possibly be land?*

This *must* be Ireland. It can be no other place than Ireland. Below me lies a great tapering bay; a long, bouldered island; a village. Yes, there's a place on the chart where it all fits—line of ink on line of shore—Valentia and Dingle Bay, *on the southwestern coast of Ireland!*

I'm almost exactly on my route, closer than I hoped to come in my wildest dreams back in San Diego.

The coast of England is well above the horizon when I see its outline, pale and whitish in the haze. How foreign—how different from America it is, with its neat, miniature farms all divided off by hedge and stone fences, and its narrow, sod-walled roads running crookedly between slate-roofed villages! How can a farmer make his living from fields so small?

There's the English Channel already—shoreline darkening against pale gray of distant water. I've crossed England so quickly! It seems so small! This is the last water, this little strip of ocean. In less than half an hour I'll be in sight of France.

A strip of land, ten miles or so in width, dents the horizon —Cape de la Hague. The coast of *France!* It comes like an outstretched hand to meet me, glowing in the light of sunset.

Almost 3500 miles from New York. I've broken the world's distance record for a nonstop airplane flight.

I'm still flying at 4000 feet when I see it, that scarcely perceptible glow, as though the moon had rushed ahead of schedule. Paris is rising over the edge of the earth. Gradually avenues, parks, and buildings take outline form; and there, far below, a little offset from the center, is a column of lights pointing upward, changing angles as I fly—the Eiffel Tower. I circle once above it, and turn northeastward toward Le Bourget [airfield].

Yes, there's a black patch to my left, large enough to be an airport. Are those floodlights, in one corner of the dark area? If they are, they're awfully weak. They're hardly bright enough to be for landing aircraft. I circle. Yes. It's definitely an airport.

I circle several times while I lose altitude. My landing direction will be over the floodlights, angling away from the hangar line. I'm wide awake, but the feel of my plane has not returned. My movements are mechanical, uncoordinated, as though I were coming down at the end of my first solo.

Bank around for final glide. Is my nose down far enough?

Yes, the air speed's at 90 miles an hour. I'll overshoot if I keep on at this rate . . . Stick back—trim the stabilizer back another notch—close the throttle—I can hardly hear the engine idling —is it too slow?—It mustn't stop now—The silence is like vacuum in my ears.

In spite of my speed, the *Spirit of St. Louis* seems about to stall. My lack of feel alarms me. I've never tried to land a plane without feel before.

I'm too high—too fast. Drop wing—left rudder—sideslip . . . Careful—mustn't get anywhere near the stall. I've never landed the *Spirit of St. Louis* at night before. The wheels touch gently—off again—No, I'll keep contact—Ease the stick forward . . . Back on the ground—Off—Back—the tail skid too —Not a bad landing, but I'm beyond the light—can't see anything ahead.

I start to taxi back toward the floodlights and hangars—But the entire field ahead is covered with running figures!

I had barely cut the engine switch when the first people reached my cockpit. Within seconds my open windows were blocked with faces. My name was called out over and over again . . . I could feel the *Spirit of St. Louis* tremble with the pressure of the crowd.

Roosevelt Field, Long Island, New York, to Le Bourget Aerodrome, Paris, France: 33 hrs. 30 min. (Fuselage fabric badly torn by souvenir hunters. Also, fairing strips broken and one grease reservoir torn off engine. Fuselage repaired and recovered at Le Bourget.)

10. Amelia Earhart on a Woman's Two Atlantic Crossings

My meeting with Captain Railey was very interesting. He told me that a woman had planned to make a transatlantic flight, but for various personal reasons she had abandoned the idea of going herself. She still, however, wanted an American to be the first of her sex to cross the ocean by air.

I went to New York as a candidate to be looked over. It was made clear that the men in the flight were being paid. I was asked if I was prepared to receive no remuneration myself. I said "Yes," feeling that the privilege of being included in the expedition would be sufficient in itself. Ultimately, Bill Stultz, the pilot, received $20,000 and Lou Gordon, the mechanic, $5000.

It took us twenty hours and forty minutes to cross from Trepassey Bay [Newfoundland] to Burrport, Wales. In Trepassey there was plenty of trouble. Weather and mechanical difficulties combined to keep us in the hamlet for thirteen days, instead of two or three as we had counted upon. So long did we linger that the natives began to think the *Friendship* couldn't fly.

Unless the wind blows from a certain direction, Trepassey harbor is too narrow for takeoff with a heavy load. About eleven on the morning of June 17th [1928], the wind was reasonably right, and the weather forecast not too unpromising. We taxied to the end of the harbor and faced into position before the wind. With the waves pounding the pontoons and breaking over the [wing] motors, we made the long trip down its length, the ship too heavy to rise. Stultz turned around and taxied back to try again.

I was crowded in the cabin with a stopwatch in my hand to check the takeoff time, and with my eyes glued on the airspeed indicator as it slowly climbed. If it passed fifty miles an

The *Friendship*. (*Library of Congress*)

hour, chances were the *Friendship* could pull out and fly. Thirty—forty—the *Friendship* was trying again. A long pause, then the pointer went to fifty. Fifty, fifty-five—sixty. We were off at last, staggering under the weight carried with the two sputtering [wing] motors which had received a thorough dousing of salt water.

Our Atlantic crossing was literally a voyage in the clouds. Incidentally the saying about their silver linings is pure fiction. The internals of most clouds are anything but silvery—they are clammy grey wetness as dismally forbidding as any one can imagine.

I kept a log of the *Friendship* flight and find I mention clouds more often than anything else. Some of the clouds held rain, and every time the plane plowed through them the [wing] motors would cough and complain. They did not like being wet because they had been caked with salt water on the takeoff and the salt had dried to make a contact for the sparks to jump from the plugs.

Eleven thousand feet, as morning came, was not high enough to climb over the clouds piled like fantastic gobs of mashed potatoes. Bill Stultz checked his gasoline and concluded we should waste too much if he went higher in an effort to surmount them. So the nose of the *Friendship* burrowed down into the white clouds and we descended quickly through the grey wetness to about 2500 feet.

Log book: "Instrument flying. Slow descent first. Going down fast. It takes a lot to make my ears hurt. 5000 now. Awfully wet. Water dripping in window."

The reference to my ears hurting simply records a rather swift descent. When a plane comes down, it necessarily enters air which grows more dense near the earth's surface. The increased pressure is noticed most on the eardrum.

85

Suddenly out of the fog, on a patch of sea beneath us, appeared a big transatlantic vessel. We circled around the vessel, hoping that the captain would guess what we wanted and have the bearings painted on the deck for us to read. But nothing happened. Then I wrote out a request that he do so, put the note into a bag with a couple of oranges for ballast, and tried to drop it on the deck. But my amateur bombing did not work; the two oranges landed in the water some distance from the ship.

So we kept on eastward.

As it turned out, we were within a few miles of the mainland when we sighted the [ship]. Though we did not know it, Ireland had been passed and we were nearing Wales. Soon after the fruitless orange bombing, we saw several fishing vessels so small that we knew they could not be many miles offshore. What shore we did not know—or care.

Just as the [ship] had loomed out of the fog, so land appeared. In the previous hours we had seen so many dark clouds which looked like land that at first we thought this new shape was simply more shadow geography.

Very low we skirted the cliffs against which the sea was beating, and looked down on a story-book countryside of neatly kept hedges, compact fields, and roadways lined with trees.

The *Friendship* had to follow water, for being fitted with pontoons, we did not dare cross large areas of unfamiliar land. After some minutes of cruising along the shore, we came to what seemed a break in the channel we were following and decided to descend near a little town. It would not be possible to take off again with the quantity of fuel we had left. So low it was by this time that the engines were supplied only when we were flying level.

Stultz set the *Friendship* down in mid-channel and taxied to a heavy marking buoy, to which the men made the plane fast. Then, having crossed the Atlantic by air, we waited for the village to come out and welcome us.

There were three men working on the railroad along the water's edge. They looked us over, waded down to the shore, and then calmly turned their backs and went to work again.

After a while, groups of people slowly gathered in the rain. Slim Gordon crawled out on the pontoons and called for a boat, to no avail.

"I'll get a boat," I said finally, and squeezed forward into the cockpit. Out of the open window I waved a white towel as a sign of distress. At my gesture a friendly gentleman on shore took off his coat and waved cordially back at me. But that was all.

Finally boats did begin to come out.

When we landed my entire baggage consisted of two scarfs, a toothbrush, and a comb. The absence of baggage—even a change of clothes—seemed to provoke much interest, especially among women. I had no intention whatever of trying to set a fashion in transatlantic air attire. My traveling wardrobe was due entirely to the necessity of economizing in weight and space.

To me, it was genuinely surprising what a disproportion of attention was given to the woman member of the *Friendship* crew at the expense of the men, who were really responsible for the flight. The credit belongs to them and to the flight's backer as well as to the manufacturers of the plane and motors.

But I happened to be a woman and the first to make a transatlantic crossing by air, and the press and the public seemed to be more interested in that fact than any other. I think in the future, as women become better able to pull their own weight in all kinds of expeditions, the fact of their sex will loom less large when credit is given for accomplishment.

*

Starting from Harbor Grace, Newfoundland, on the afternoon of May 20, 1932, I landed near Londonderry in the north of Ireland the next morning, thirteen and a half hours after the takeoff. That, briefly, is the story of my solo flight across the Atlantic.

Ever since my first crossing in the *Friendship,* in 1928, when I was merely a passenger, I have wanted to attempt a solo flight. Then, a few months ago I decided upon it seriously.

It was clear in my mind that I was undertaking the flight because I loved flying. I chose to fly the Atlantic because I wanted to. It was, in a measure, a self-justification—a proving to me, and to anyone else interested, that a woman with adequate experience could do it.

First [Bernt] Balchen and his helpers strengthened the fuselage of the Lockheed, which had had some hard knocks in the three years I have flown it. Then extra fuel tanks were put in the wings and a large tank installed in the cabin. Additional instruments were installed, including a drift indicator and additional compasses. From Pratt & Whitney in Hartford I secured a new "Wasp" motor, for my old one had flown a bit too long for the Atlantic grind.

In the meanwhile, as opportunity offered, I would drive over from my home at Rye and get in odd hours in the air. Most of these were devoted to blind flying until I felt really confident of my ability to handle the ship without looking outside of the cockpit—that is, flying it solely with instruments.

On Friday, the 20th [of May] we took off. Three hours and thirty minutes later we were. at St. John, New Brunswick.

Bernt Balchen, Amelia Earhart, Eddie Gorski, in 1932. (*Smithsonian Institution*)

Early the next morning we flew to Harbor Grace in New-foundland, arriving at 2:15 P.M. I left Bernt and Eddie [Gor-ski] checking ship and motor while I found a friendly bed and restful nap. In ample time I was awakened.

At the field, the engine was warmed up. A final message from my husband was handed to me. I shook hands with Bernt and Eddie, and climbed into the cockpit. The southwest wind was nearly right for the runway. At twelve minutes after seven, I gave her the gun. The plane gathered speed, and despite the heavy load rose easily.

For several hours there was fair weather with a lingering sunset. And then the moon came up over a low bank of clouds. For those first hours I was flying about 12,000 feet. And then something happened that has never occurred in my twelve years of flying. The altimeter, the instrument which records height above ground, failed. Suddenly the hands swung around the dial uselessly and I knew the instrument was out of commission for the rest of the flight.

About 11:30, the moon disappeared behind some clouds, and I ran into rather a severe storm with lightning, and I was considerably buffeted about, and with difficulty held my course. Once I saw the moon for a fleeting instant and thought I could pull out on top of the clouds, so I climbed for half an hour when suddenly I realized I was picking up ice.

I knew by the climb of the ship, which was not as fast as usual, that it was accumulating a weight of ice. Then I saw slush on the windowpane. In addition, ice began to coat my air-speed indicator so that it refused to register accurately on the panel before me.

In such a situation one has to get into warmer air, so I went down, hoping the ice would melt. I descended until I could see the waves breaking although I could not tell exactly how far I was above them. I kept flying there until fog came down so low that I dared not keep on at such an altitude.

There was nothing left but to seek a middle ground, that is, to fly under the altitude at which I picked up ice and over the water by a sufficient margin. This would have been much easier to do had I been able to know my height.

Later, I tried going up again with the same result. So I gave up, just plowing through the "soup" and not looking out of the cockpit again until morning came.

About four hours out of Newfoundland, I noticed a small blue flame licking through a broken weld in the [engine's] manifold ring. I knew that it would grow worse as the night wore on. However, the metal was very heavy and I hoped it would last until I reached land.

As daylight dawned, I found myself between two layers of clouds, the first very high, probably 20,000 feet, the lower ones little fluffy white clouds near the water. Soon I ran into another bank of clouds. I was in these for at least an hour and then came out in a clear space again. By this time, the upper layer was thin enough for the sun to come through, and it was as dazzling as on real snow. I had dark glasses but it was too much for me even so, and I came down through the lower layer to fly in the shade, as it were.

By the way, I didn't bother much about food for myself. The really important thing was fuel for the engine. It drank more than 300 gallons of gasoline. My own transatlantic rations consisted of one can of tomato juice which I punctured and sipped through a straw.

The last two hours were the hardest. My exhaust manifold was vibrating very badly, and then I turned on the reserve tanks and found the gauge leaking. I decided I should come down at the very nearest place, wherever it was.

I think I hit Ireland about the middle. I started down the coast and found thunderstorms in the hills. Not having the altimeter and not knowing the country, I was afraid to plow through those lest I hit one of the mountains, so I turned north where the weather seemed to be better and soon came across a railroad, which I followed, hoping it would lead me to a city, where there might be an airport.

The first place I encountered was Londonderry, and I circled it hoping to locate a landing field but found lovely pastures instead. I succeeded in frightening all the cattle in the county, I think, as I came down low several times before finally landing in a long, sloping meadow. I couldn't have asked for better landing facilities.

11. Curtis E. LeMay
on Finding the *Rex*

[Ira] Eaker decided that the range and capability of the B-17 could be brought strikingly to the public attention. A famous passenger liner was to be selected as a theoretical enemy vessel and was to be intercepted at sea.

The Italian liner *Rex* got the nod. She would be inbound on the 12th of May, perhaps 700 miles out east of New York harbor.

From the start there burgeoned an ambitious but somewhat risky plan. It had been decided that a complement of newspaper reporters and radio broadcasters would be invited to come along in the three B-17's. Since C.V. [Haynes] was to fly lead, that meant that I would be lead navigator for the project.

Some of Ira Eaker's boys had gone around to call on Italian steamship company officials when this idea was dreamed up initially. The Italians agreed to cooperate, with alacrity. No doubt they had visions of profitable publicity as a result of radio broadcasts and news stories which would ensue—granted that the proposed rendezvous was kept. The name *Rex* would appear in a thousand headlines and—the steamship people hoped—hordes of tourists would come elbowing aboard on future voyages.

The three Forts to be engaged in this search would move over to Mitchel Field on Long Island the night before the exercise took place. Thus reporters and radio people could come out to Mitchel in the early morning and board the airplanes there. Our crew in No. 80 would be hosts to the NBC representatives—two radio technicians and an announcer. Newspaper reporters would travel on the other planes.

Lieutenant Curtis E. LeMay. (*U.S. Air Force*)

May 11th was a Wednesday. When we got over to Mitchel along in the middle of the afternoon, there arrived a radiogram from the *Rex.* They had sent their noontime position. We would be finding the *Rex*—if we did find her—away south of Nova Scotia. For that area, Weather kept coming up with ominous forecasts of low ceilings, increased precipitation, etc.

To this day I don't know why the *Rex* didn't send us their position report that night, but we never received it.

Some of the rest of the people may have slept; I couldn't sleep. With the first paleness of daylight I heard a gusty rain slapping at the windows. I got up, chilly and dejected, and took a look. It resembled some of that good old Air Mail Weather. I dressed and tried to eat, but—Bah. The rest were in the same condition.

It was an errand of courtesy for us to go up to headquarters and meet our guests and passengers. The other two navigators and I didn't hang around there long, however. We wanted to go over to Weather, and also we were in a tizzy about that *Rex* position. By this time, certainly, the latest position report should have been relayed to us. The steamship company had promised faithfully to send it over at least by midnight.

No report whatsoever. One sergeant had been calling the steamship office perpetually, and nobody answered, not even a janitor. It was around eight o'clock in the morning now. I started thinking about a broadcast to be made from our airplane when we met up with an object exactly 879 feet and nine inches long, out there in bad weather on the stormy Atlantic *that very noon.* My stomach turned over.

Weather report as follows: a cold front was barricading our entire route. There would be all sorts of turbulence. Heavy precipitation was forecast. Ahead of this front there was also intense shower activity. Ceilings would be down to nothing in the area where it was hoped we could find the steamship.

Next thing I knew, C.V. Haynes was standing beside me. I asked him what time he planned to take off.

He glanced at his wristwatch. "Something like twenty-nine minutes from now. Eight-thirty, to be exact."

All the hopelessness which I felt was reflected in Haynes' own face, as in a sad gray mirror. "Curt, can you figure out —If the *Rex* is on her normal course, do you have an idea what time we'll encounter her? We've *got* to know."

I leaned over the counter and went to work. Before long I had an answer for C.V. "I make it twelve twenty-five," I told him. "That's provided she's on course."

*

One by one the twelve engines on the three Forts came thunderingly alive. C.V. started to taxi, then slowed down. Next thing our hatch was opened, and eventually a wet scrap of paper made its way into my hands. Our laggardly Italian friends had finally come through with the latest coordinates of the *Rex.* And the best sprinter at Operations had caught up with us, with not a second to spare.

C.V. poured on the coal. Next minute we were bucking aloft through the murk, and I was hanging on to my desk with one hand and trying to jot down figures with the other.

Immediately I saw that the *Rex* wasn't nearly as close in as we had expected her to be.

C.V. Haynes had asked for an ETA [estimated time of arrival] in that area, and I had given it to him. He'd said, "We've *got* to know." And I had said 12:25 and now an awful suspicion was plaguing me. I had a hunch why Haynes had demanded that I give him an ETA at that particular moment.

We passed over Sandy Hook at 0845, then the storms

claimed us. Most of the time we couldn't even see the water, and turbulence was heaving us all over the sky.

Frequently I have been asked about the altitude on which we were proceeding on this trip, and people rather blink when I give them the honest answer: "All the way from six hundred to six thousand feet." I have been in a great deal of turbulence through some thirteen thousand hours of military flying. I doubt that we ever flew in worse turbulence than on that 12th of May [1938].

Good thing that Haynes had a massive pair of shoulders, and powerful arms. It was as if a giant clung to the other end of that control column and kept trying to wrench it away from C.V. I don't know how many thunderstorms were around; maybe a dozen. We kept turning and twisting, trying to avoid the worst turbulence in these, and were changing altitude constantly. Didn't dare lose complete contact with the water, for I had to measure our drift.

Then I calculated the head wind, which was infinitely more intense than in the forecast given us by Weather. Our ground speed was at least ten knots slower than predicted.

Vince Meloy made his way up out of the waist where he had been reassuring a very apprehensive radio crew. He was hanging on to anything which could be hung on to. He shouted in my direction—at first I didn't know what he was yelling—perhaps he was telling me that the radio people were airsick, as who shouldn't be?

But his next words came screeching remotely into my ears. Sounded like: "NBC will broadcast at 12:25 . . . There'll be millions of listeners."

"But at 12:25—" I was gasping for breath. "Why does it have to be at 12:25?"

"That was your estimate. You said we'd encounter the *Rex* at that time."

I crept over to C.V. Haynes' seat, and hung there while I tried to yell in his ear and explain the exact situation. We plunged into another line squall. Our pilot was fighting wheel and column while he tried to listen to me.

"You're the navigator, Curt," was the best I could get out of him.

I tottered back to my own position, and picked up a pencil; shook the charts, tried to blow the water off. I went to work once more.

The cockpit area darkened. I looked out to see what in——

We had a great big dusky wall looming ahead of us. That was the cold front. Above the growl of the four engines, above all the banging and crashing and clanking, and distant quacking of radio voices . . . yes, C.V. was telling Smith and Cousland, in 82 and 81, respectively, to move out on his wing in order to penetrate the front individually.

Boom. We went into that Maytime cold front like a bullet going into a backstop on the target range. It took us about ten minutes to get through the front. Haynes might as well have been rolling all over the mat with Strangler Lewis. But he won, Ma. We felt like slapping him on the shoulders to indicate that fall was his.

We came out into bright sunshine. C.V. called in the other airplanes. Soon as they had rejoined us, I asked him to fly another series of turns. Again and again I checked: there seemed to be nothing wrong with my results. There was no longer any safety margin, but the present course should bring us into a perfect interception of the liner. *If* I was correct in my calculations.

It had all been dead reckoning; there were no cities or rivers or any other landmarks underneath—only thousands of square miles of agitated water.

We were now flying the three Forts in a 30-mile broad search band. Still, 30 miles was a narrow little ribbon when extended against those tossing empty masses of gray swells and torn spume.

Looked at my watch. 12:21. Sunlight vanished, again we were in the clutch of a squall; the rain beat like leaden pellets against the windows.

12:23. Columns of murky clouds split, staggered aside; we were coming out of this later squall, we could even see the ocean.

12:25 . . .

Dead ahead was the Italian liner: a toy beauty, neat and proud and compact. We could even see the fat bands of red, white, and green encircling her thick modern funnels. Yes, this was the *Rex*. We didn't have to come close enough to read

B-17's intercept the *Rex,* 776 miles at sea. (*U.S. Air Force*)

the golden name emblazoned on her bows in order to know that.

Now we were down there joining her, at mast level. Hundreds of passengers swarmed the decks, wrapped in raincoats and scarfs, waving madly up at us.

I still couldn't quite believe that she was there, but she was. The broadcast must be going on: the one originating in the waist of our airplane. I tried to envision all those millions of listeners, clear back across the continent, listening amiably and contentedly to that broadcast.

Actually we had a worse time weatherwise going back than we had coming out. It was getting late in the afternoon, when thunderstorms always build up in intensity. We didn't have enough gas to fly around those storms. When we hit that stuff it was rougher than ——.

The artificial horizon went blooey . . . the rate-of-climb indicator was jiggling so badly you couldn't see a thing. The bank-and-turn indicator was hitting the peg on both sides. I remember watching our air speed: it would run down to about 80 miles an hour, then up to about 240. Old No. 80 banged and trembled as if she were coming apart at the seams.

At times on that return to land we began to wonder whether we'd really make it. It was that close.

12. Ted W. Lawson
on Launching B-25 Bombers
from an Aircraft Carrier

I heard that Davey Jones, who had been in Dayton for a couple of days with our squadron commander, Captain Edward J. York, of San Antonio, Texas, wanted to see all officers in his hotel suite. We were staying in downtown Minneapolis.

We all strolled into the big hotel suite—there were twenty-four of us—and sat around on the beds and chairs, smoking and clowning a little. Most of us forgot to look at Davey very closely.

When we were all there, Davey went around and closed the doors of the suite. When he finally spoke, he didn't raise his voice.

"I've just come back from talking with Captain York," Davey said, quietly. "There's been a change. We're not going to work out of Columbia. Captain York wanted me to talk to you and see how many of you would volunteer for a special mission. It's dangerous, important, and interesting," he added, after a pause.

Lieutenant Ted W. Lawson. (*National Archives*)

One of the fellows spoke up and asked, "Well, what is it?"

"I can't tell you," Davey said. "I don't even know myself. I've got a hunch, but no real information, and I'm not talking about my hunch. All I can tell you is that it's dangerous and that it'll take you out of the country for maybe two or three months."

"Where?" somebody asked.

"I'm sorry I can't tell you any more," Davey said. "You've

heard all the particulars I can give you. Now, who'll volunteer? It's perfectly all right if you don't. It's strictly up to you."

All of us volunteered.

We were ordered to fly to Eglin Field, near Pensacola. Our crew talked a lot about that on the trip down and came to a lot of haphazard conclusions. We certainly weren't going to fly to any foreign country from Eglin, we decided. We also decided that this would be where we'd train for whatever we were going to do and that "it" had something to do with flying over water—for Eglin is near the Gulf.

Our squadron put its three-prong wheels down on Eglin on February 28th. As I taxied across the field after the landing, I looked around and saw we had company. B-25's from three more squadrons of the 17th Group were scattered around the place. There were 24 bombers in all.

They must know something, I figured, but after I had checked in and talked to some of the boys in the other squadrons I found that they were as much in the dark as we were.

So that night we sat around and buffaloed about a lot of things, mostly guessing at what was in store for us. I remember one thing that was said early in the bull session. One of the boys from another squadron said to me, "Guess who's here?"

I said I couldn't guess.

"Jimmy Doolittle," he said. "He's a Lieutenant Colonel now, and I think he's going to have a hell of a lot to say about this mission."

We met Doolittle the next day, March 1st. I had heard and read a lot about him, of course, and had seen his picture a number of times. But it was quite a shock to see how young-looking his face was after those years of stunting, barnstorming, and racing.

About 140 of us crowded into Eglin's Operations Office.

We sat on benches and windowsills and, when we were more or less quiet, Doolittle began to talk.

The first thing he said was, "If you men have any idea that this isn't the most dangerous thing you've ever been on, don't even start this training period. You can drop out now. There isn't much sense wasting time and money training men who aren't going through with this thing. It's perfectly all right for any of you to drop out."

A couple of the boys spoke up together and asked Doolittle if he could give them any information about the mission. You could hear a pin drop.

"No, I can't—just now," Doolittle said. "But you'll begin to get an idea of what it's all about the longer we're down here training for it. Now, there's one important thing I want to stress. This whole thing must be kept secret. I don't even want you to tell your wives, no matter what you see, or are asked to do, down here. If you've guessed where we're going, don't even talk about your guess. That means every one of you. Don't even talk among yourselves about this thing. Now, does anybody want to drop out?"

Nobody dropped out.

Takeoff practice started the end of the first week at Eglin. One morning Doolittle introduced us to a Lieutenant, Senior Grade, of the Navy—Lieutenant Henry L. Miller. He had come over from Pensacola and would be our special instructor in quick takeoffs. The Navy knew a lot about such things.

This practicing was done at auxiliary fields away from all eyes. Flags were placed along the white-lined runways of these fields at 200, 300, and 500 feet. The idea, we soon found out, was to get into the air in less space and time than we believed was possible for a B-25. We did this by dropping our landing flaps and pouring all the coal we could on the engines.

The mission for which we had all blindly volunteered took on shape and substance as the days passed. That we would be carted somewhere by the Navy was apparent after Lieutenant Miller lectured to us at great length on Navy courtesy and etiquette. He told us about saluting the national ensign on the stern of the ship we boarded, and gave us a glossary of nautical terms. He even told us how to take a shower bath on a ship without wasting water.

We had our only crack-up of the training period about March 15th. Lieutenant Miller, the Navy man, was in it. He was flying with Lieutenant Dick Joyce of Lincoln, Nebraska, with a load of dummy bombs and a full gas load, including the reserve tanks. It was during one of those hard-to-believe takeoffs. Joyce got the wheels off the ground and pulled them up in a hurry, but the ship wobbled and dropped back on the runway. It skidded along, shrieking, on its belly; the props, which only have a nine-inch ground clearance, chewing themselves to pieces. We held our breath, waiting for the flames. But they didn't come.

It was just a part of our education. Soon all of us were able to get our fully loaded ships off the runway at between 55 and 60 mph with full flaps, whereas the normal takeoff speed for a B-25 is 80 or 90 after a run three or four times as long.

We were given little warning before leaving Eglin. We were awakened at 3 A.M. on the morning of March 24th and told that we'd take off at 11 A.M.

I took off with five other B-25's that morning of March 24th and we flew to San Antonio. We stayed there overnight and the next day we flew on to March Field, on the Coast.

We had to fly up to Sacramento's McClellan Field from March Field as soon as we could. So we took off right after breakfast and flew up there, brushing the trees.

We spent a few more days in that area, practicing full-flap takeoffs at small, almost deserted fields. Then one morning we hopped over the hump to Alameda. We were on our way again; we had been training a month.

As I put the flaps down for the landing, we all let out a yell at the same time, and I guess we all got the same empty feeling in the stomach that I did.

An American aircraft carrier was underneath us. Three of our B-25's were already on its deck.

"Damn! Ain't she small," somebody said in the interphone.

We landed on the field and taxied over to the side where Doolittle and York were beckoning to us. I rolled back my window and looked down at them.

"Is everything O.K.?" Doolittle asked.

I said everything was.

"Taxi off the field and park at the edge of the *Hornet*'s wharf. They'll take care of you there," Doolittle said.

As soon as I did, the Navy boys jumped all over us. They drained out all our gas, except a few gallons. One of the boys got in, after our crew got out. An Army "donkey" hooked the [aircraft's] main gear and towed it down the pier. We walked down after it and then watched the claws of a big crane reach down and pick up our ship as if it weighed ten pounds. The crane swung it slowly up on the deck of the *Hornet*.

We began moving the next morning at nine o'clock. That first day I wandered through the ship with the rest of the Army fellows, figuring out how not to get lost. The Navy boys kidded us a lot, trying to get us to tell them where we were going. But we were mum. We just looked wise, as if we knew.

The word Japan was mentioned officially for the first time the next morning. Doolittle called us together in the empty mess hall and all of us sensed that now we'd know.

He cleared his throat and said, "For the benefit of those of you who don't already know, or who have been guessing, we are going straight to Japan. We're going to bomb Tokyo, Yokohama, Osaka, Kobe, and Nagoya. The Navy is going to take us in as close as is advisable, and, of course, we're going to take off from the deck."

When the meeting broke up, all of us drifted instinctively to our planes. Some of the boys walked along the flight deck, measuring off the alarmingly short distance between the island and the bow. You see, we didn't have to be told that we'd be able to use only about half the deck. We knew there wouldn't be any place to put the 16 parked planes, except to squeeze them in together on the stern. Even then we figured that they'd take up nearly half the deck. So the boys who were pacing off the probable distance we'd have for a takeoff were measuring from the middle of the island to the bow. And scratching their heads at the end of their pacing.

All of us got a scare, the third day out, that we'd miss the raid. The Navy boys came out with buckets of white paint and drew a line along the port side, two or three yards in from the edge. We heard that Doolittle had decided to send one of the planes back to the mainland with a message. The message couldn't be sent any other way because the *Hornet* was observing radio silence. I tried to keep out of Doolittle's sight as much as possible, and so did the others. The line, of course, was to be the guide of the plane ordered to take off. It was easy to figure out that the left wheel of the unlucky B-25 selected would have to keep on that line. In order to clear the island with the tip of the right wing, the fuselage of the plane had to be quite far over to the left, and the left wing would extend out over the edge of the ship.

Our fears subsided after the line was drawn. A Navy blimp

came over to us, hovered over the deck, dropped us some stuff, and presumably took back the necessary messages that had to be transmitted to the mainland. It was a relief to know that I hadn't gone through all that training just to become a messenger boy.

We swung readily into the Navy routine. Twice a day over the loudspeakers would come the nasal command, "General quarters! Man your battle stations!" It usually came just before dawn and at dusk. Wherever we were and whatever we were doing, we'd scramble up the ladders and passageways and take our posts.

We were more than spectators at these drills. Doolittle had told us in one of the meetings that if we were attacked from the air we would have to get our planes off the deck in a hurry, and, with that in mind, we always knew just where we were and the direction and distance of the closest friendly land. If we were attacked by a surface vessel, particularly at long range, we were to leave the planes where they were and depend on the *Hornet*'s guns and the heavier guns of the accompanying warships.

Gasoline was my main worry toward the end. I would lie in my bunk with an ear-splitting card game going on in the same room until the small hours of the morning, and the thought of getting enough gas in my ship would never leave my mind.

So I went to Doolittle one day toward the end and told him that I had been figuring our probable gas consumption and asked him if I could carry 25 five-gallon cans in the plane instead of the ten he had allotted us. I told him I realized that the extra gas would weigh six pounds a gallon but that I was sure my ship could take it.

"No," he said. "Your tail might get sluggish with that extra four hundred and fifty pounds in there. It might start whipping around, and there's not going to be a lot of room to do that. The first important thing you've got to do is get off this deck. If you can't do that, well, we will have wasted a helluva lot of time and money."

It was about 7:30 A.M. [April 18, 1942], bitterly cold and rough. That's when it happened. First there was a muffled, vibrating roar, followed immediately by the husky cry of battle stations.

We were three decks down. Scrambling as fast as I could, I found other Army boys racing for the top. We flung questions at one another, but got no answers. And twice before I could get up on top, the *Hornet* vibrated and echoed with the sound of heavy gunfire near by.

I got out on the flight deck and ran around a B-25 just in time to see the cruiser off to our left let go another broadside of flame in the direction away from us. And presently, down near the horizon, a low-slung ship began to give off an ugly plume of black smoke. Dive bombers were wheeling over it.

I must have asked two dozen questions in one minute. One of the Navy boys, hurrying past, said it was a Japanese patrol boat and that our gunnery had accounted for it within three minutes after engaging.

This was it, and before we wanted it. We'd have to take off now. Not Sunday evening. Now, Saturday morning. We were forced to assume that the Japanese ship had had time to flash the warning about us. All hope of surprising the Japanese had now fled, I thought. Surprise was our main safety factor, Doolittle had often drummed into our heads.

Now we were going to take off about 800 miles off the coast. It took some figuring—quick figuring. And the sums I arrived at, in my buzzing head, gave me a sudden emptiness in the stomach.

"Army pilots, man your planes! Army pilots, man your planes!" the loudspeakers brayed. But I already knew the time had come.

The Navy was now taking charge, and doing it with an efficiency which made our popped eyes pop some more. Blocks were whipped out from under wheels. The whirring little "donkey" was pushing and pulling the B-25's into position.

In about half an hour the Navy had us criss-crossed along the back end of the flight deck, two abreast, the big double-rudder tail assemblies of the 16 planes sticking out of the edges of the rear of the ship at an angle. From the air, the *Hornet,* with its slim, clean foredeck, and its neatly cluttered rear deck, must have looked like an arrow with pinfeathers bounding along the surface of the water.

It was good enough flying weather, but the sea was tremendous. The *Hornet* bit into the rough-house waves, dipping and rising until the flat deck was a crazy seesaw. Some of the waves actually were breaking over the deck. The deck seemed to grow smaller by the minute, and I had a brief fear of being hit by a wave on the takeoff and of crashing at the end of the deck and falling off into the path of the careening carrier.

The *Hornet*'s speed rose until it was making its top speed, that hectic, hurried, perfect morning of April 18th. The bombs now came up from below and rolled along the deck on their low-slung lorries to our planes.

The *Hornet*'s control tower was now beginning to display large square cards, giving us compass readings and the wind, which was of gale proportions.

Doolittle warmed and idled his engines, and now we got a vivid demonstration of one of our classroom lectures on how to get a 25,000-pound bomber off half the deck of a carrier.

A Navy man stood at the bow of the ship, and off to the left, with a checkered flag in his hand. He gave Doolittle, who was at the controls, the signal to begin racing his engines again. He did it by swinging the flag in a circle and making it go faster and faster. Doolittle gave his engines more and more throttle until I was afraid that he'd burn them up. A wave crashed heavily at the bow and sprayed the deck.

Then I saw that the man with the flag was waiting, timing the dipping of the ship so that Doolittle's plane would get the benefit of a rising deck for its takeoff. Then the man gave a new signal. Navy boys pulled the blocks from under Doolittle's wheels. Another signal and Doolittle released his brakes and the bomber moved forward.

With full flaps, motors at full throttle, and his left wing far out over the port side of the *Hornet,* Doolittle's plane waddled and then lunged slowly into the teeth of the gale that swept down the deck. His left wheel stuck on the white line as if it were a track. His right wing, which had barely cleared the wall of the island as he taxied and was guided up to the starting line, extended nearly to the edge of the starboard side.

We watched him like hawks, wondering what the wind would do to him, and whether we could get off in that little run toward the bow. If he couldn't, we couldn't.

Doolittle picked up more speed and held to his line, and, just as the *Hornet* lifted itself up on the top of a wave and cut through it at full speed, Doolittle's plane took off. He had yards to spare. He hung his ship almost straight up on its props, until we could see the whole top of his B-25. Then he

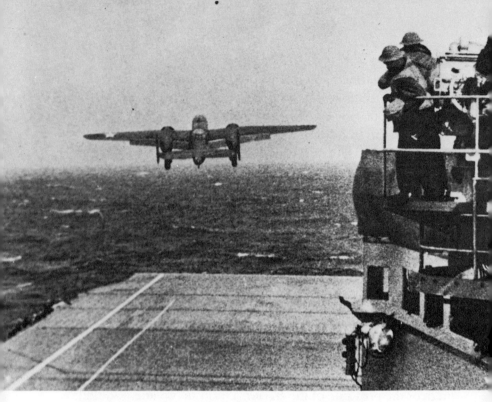

B-25 launches from U.S.S. *Hornet*. (*U.S. Air Force*)

leveled off and I watched him come around in a tight circle and shoot low over our heads—straight down the line painted on the deck.

The *Hornet* was giving him his bearings. Admiral Halsey had headed it for the heart of Tokyo.

The engines of three other ships were warming up, and the thump and hiss of the turbulent sea made additional noise. But loud and clear above those sounds I could hear the hoarse cheers of every Navy man on the ship. They made the *Hornet* fairly shudder with their yells—and I've never heard anything like it, before or since.

Travis Hoover went off second and nearly crashed. Brick Holstrom was third; Bob Gray, fourth; Davey Jones, fifth; Dean Hallmark, sixth; and I was seventh.

I was on the line now, my eyes glued on the man with the flag. He gave me the signal to put my flaps down. I reached down and drew the flap lever back and down. I checked the electrical instrument that indicates whether the flaps are working. They were. I could feel the plane quaking with the strain of having the flat surface of the flaps thrust against the gale and the blast from the props. I got a sudden fear that they might blow off and cripple us, so I pulled up the flaps again, and I guess the Navy man understood. He let it go and began giving me the signal to rev my engines.

I liked the way they sounded long before he did. There had been a moment, earlier, when I had an agonizing fear that something was wrong with the left engine. It wouldn't start, at first. But I had gotten it going, good. Now, after fifteen seconds of watching the man with the flag spinning his arm faster and faster, I began to worry again. He must know his stuff, I tried to tell myself, but when, for God's sake, would he let me go?

I thought of all the things that could go wrong at this last minute. Our instructions along these lines were simple and to the point. If a motor quit or caught fire, if a tire went flat, if the right wing badly scraped the island, if the left wheel went over the edge, we were to get out as quickly as we could and help the Navy shove our $150,000 plane overboard. It must not, under any circumstances, be permitted to block traffic. There would be no other way to clear the forward deck for the other planes to take off.

After 30 blood-sweating seconds the Navy man was satisfied with the sound of my engines. Our wheel blocks were jerked out, and when I released the brakes we quivered forward, the wind grabbing at the wings. We rambled dangerously close to the edge, but I braked in time, got the left wheel back on the white line and picked up speed. The *Hornet*'s deck bucked wildly. A sheet of spray rushed back at us.

I never felt the takeoff. One moment the end of the *Hornet*'s flight deck was rushing at us alarmingly fast; the next split second I glanced down hurriedly at what had been a white line, and it was water. There was no drop nor any surge into the air. I just went off at deck level and pulled out in front of the great ship that had done its best to plant us in Japan's front yard.

I banked now, gaining a little altitude, and instinctively reached down to pull up the flaps. With a start I realized that they were not down. I had taken off without using them.

I swung around as Doolittle and the others before me had done, came over the nine remaining planes on the deck, got the bearing and went on—hoping the others would get off and that the *Hornet*—God rest her—would get away in time.

13. Jacqueline Cochran Odlum on Setting Flying Records

A woman in the air had the choice of flying around in a light plane for pleasure or of obtaining for herself new fast and experimental equipment and determining the maximum that could be obtained from its use. I followed the second course. The objective in each flight was to go faster or farther through the atmosphere or higher into it than anyone else and to bring back some new information about plane, engine, fuel, instruments, air, or pilot that would be helpful in the conquest of the atmosphere.

For more than twenty years I have been exploring the atmosphere, with racing and flying for international speed records as the motivation. I have flown seven races and have gone after new records more than seventy times. Except for the London-Melbourne Race I did all this racing and record flying solo without copilot or other crew member.

Were I to make the simple statement that I climbed to an

altitude of 33,000 feet, that statement in and of itself would mean nothing because I have often gone higher than that. But when I add that I did this in 1937 in a fabric-covered biplane without heating, without pressurization, and without an oxygen mask, the elements of an accomplishment are added.

I nearly froze; the pipestem between my teeth through which I tried to get an oxygen supply from a tank and connecting tube was inadequate for the purpose, and I became so disoriented through lack of oxygen that it took over an hour to get my bearings and make a landing.

I never could ponder over the risks too much because I had to take a fast plane whenever it became available to me and make the best of it. I won the 1938 Bendix Race in a Seversky pursuit plane which I had never flown until that night. It was

Jacqueline Cochran congratulated by Bendix (left) and Seversky. (*U.S. Air Force*)

a prototype that had not yet been tested. I tested it en route during the race.

Its feature was that it had wings that were in effect integrated tanks so that most of the wings could be filled with fuel, thus adding range. It developed in flight that the fuel from the right wing would not properly feed the engine. By force on the stick I had to hold that wing much higher than the other from time to time in order to drain the fuel from that right wing into the left wing and from that left wing into the engine.

When I got the plane back to the factory after the race a large wad of wrapping paper was discovered near the outlet of the right-wing tank. No wonder the drainage was bad. Likely it was paper pasted on the inside of the wing during manufacture which had not been removed and which worked loose from the action of the gasoline and the vibration of the plane.

Another Bendix Race—the one in 1946—provided an abundance of memorable experiences. That was the first race following the war and was to be a battle between various makes of fighter aircraft, particularly the Mustang, the Lightning, and the Thunderbolt.

I bought a surplus Mustang (F-51) off the government stockpile for $3000. The idea was to take the machine guns out of the wing emplacements and to convert the wings into fuel tanks by giving them a plastic coating on the inner sides to make them hold gasoline. The other leading competitors with Mustangs did this but I was late in getting my Mustang and there was no time for such work.

So I decided to carry exterior drop tanks. They would slow me up by about 40 miles an hour until dropped, but in case of no wind or a head wind I could make this up after the dropping because I would have more fuel in reserve than the others and in consequence could pull more power.

To get an extra amount of fuel I decided to use, not the drop tanks that were made for the Mustang, but the larger, longer drop tanks that were made for use on the Lightning. The air suction was so great between these long tanks and the nearby landing wheels on my plane that if I waited after takeoff until the spinning of the wheels had slowed down I could not get the gear up at all. I made, in consequence, a very dramatic takeoff because the onlookers saw my landing gear go into retraction at the very second that I became airborne.

Nothing happened until I reached the border between California and Arizona. At that point my radio went dead in the middle of a check I was making on weather ahead. I turned and twirled and twisted everything connected with that radio to try to get it back into operation. Finally in anger and despair I gave it a good hard kick with my foot. All I got out of this was a very sore toe.

There was bad weather in the Grand Canyon area. I was flying at 24,000 feet and thought I could top the storm in front by climbing to 30,000 feet. But when I got to 27,000 feet the engine quit. Then it started. It surged on and off and on and off. This started my plane swinging backward and forward in the sky as if it were the seat of a swing attached to ropes several miles long. It so happened that the particular engine while being operated above 27,000 feet was subject to what is technically known as "cavitation," which is evidenced by a surging of power due to faulty utilization of the fuel.

I had no choice but to turn the nose of the plane down and head into that storm on instruments. I hit that front going full speed and while still rocking. Going on instruments under normal flight conditions is fairly routine procedure, but doing so suddenly with the plane swinging so much as to be almost out of control was somewhat like diving into a pool of cold water from a platform that is on a long pole swinging in the breeze. The instruments finally indicated that the plane was stabilized and within a few minutes I was beyond the storm. But trouble was not over.

The exterior tanks were such a drag on speed that they had to be detached and dropped as soon as empty. It was necessary to drop them before getting over populated areas. So I pulled the tank release controls while still over the mountain country and when they still carried fuel. The plane made a violent jerk —almost like a collision in the air.

The front ends of the tanks dropped away from the plane's wings while the rear ends remained fastened. The airstream caught the front ends with violence and swung them down, as a result of which the rear ends swiveled up and hit the trailing edges of my wings. These trailing edges were badly crumpled and torn in this collision between tanks and wings.

I reached the finish line six minutes behind the winner to take second place. The head wind I had hoped for turned out to be a tail wind and cost me more than six minutes. The damaged wings cost me at least another ten minutes. So, all in all, I considered it a very successful day.

I had the first homing device ever put in a private plane. It never worked properly but partly as a result of my reports subsequent ones did. I had the first turbo supercharger ever installed in a private plane. It blew up and wrecked my plane. But better ones were built and became standard equipment.

In competition everything is pushed to the limit or beyond. After the 1946 Bendix Race the chief pilot for one of the airlines asked me how high the engine temperature went. My reply was that I deliberately refrained from looking at the temperature gauge during the entire flight because I knew I had to fly with everything pretty much wide open and I did not want to get distracted by seeing needles on the dials pointing in the wrong direction.

These races and record flights were full of adventure but they do not crowd out of my memory the many wonderful experiences I have had during thousands of hours of poky air jaunts. My flying has been my passport to many wonderful places.

Not the least of these memorable places has been way up high in the sky above the murky dust-laden air that hugs the earth. The sun at twilight from up there seems twice as bright and warm while rolling over the horizon with a smiling good night. The stars seem to hold their distance from the plane by only a mile or two. I have chased many a rainbow through the heavens and I have also chased a moon bow.

The northern lights I have seen on more than one occasion. The St. Elmo lights are like immediate insistent devil children of the northern lights sent down to plague and to scare. Sometimes these lights will circle the nose of the plane or the propeller tips and follow along with the plane in flight. Sometimes they will roll over the leading edges of the wings and off the tips like balls of fire. I had no warning when I first met up with these freaks of electricity and my thoughts weren't pleasant. But the St. Elmo lights are harmless to plane and occupants and when this is known become an enjoyable occasional flight phenomenon.

The world is full of interesting places and some of the ones that are inaccessible to the ordinary traveler I have seen. I made a flight for quite a distance north over the polar ice cap . . . down in the Grand Canyon below the rim . . . around the

Canadian F-86 Sabre-jet MK III. (*Canadair*)

crater of the volcano Vesuvius . . . around the Taj Mahal by full moonlight.

Canadair, Ltd., was making Sabre-jet planes in Montreal for the United States, British, and Canadian Air Forces. It was the fastest model of the Sabre-jet, the only one that could pass the sonic barrier even in a full-power dive. The Canadian authorities were about to try out a Canadian-designed and built Orenda engine in the Sabre-jet.

I was hired by Canadair as a flight consultant [in 1953]. I had five short flights in that Sabre-jet plane before I flew it around the 100-kilometer course for a new world's record— for man as well as woman.

The 100-kilometer course was circular and around 12 pylons. The height of flight above the course was 300 feet—this low in order that the photographic timing device would catch me accurately as I passed the start and finish points of the circuit.

"Chuck" Yeager was in a chase plane to act as observer

around the course. I had fuel enough at full power to fly the course twice, provided I would turn onto course promptly after takeoff and land immediately after completion of the speed run. That would give me a margin of two minutes of fuel.

On my first run I obtained 652 and a fraction miles per hour. On my second run I was a mile per hour slower. The first run was naturally taken for certification of record to the Federation Aeronautique Internationale in Paris.

The following week a morning opened up with conditions satisfactory, except for a 15-knot wind, and I went around the course five times for a 500-kilometer record of 590 miles per hour.

There were two more records I wanted to try for—the 15-kilometer straightaway and the 3-kilometer straightaway. Finally June 2 opened up with weather that was not good but was flyable.

At ten o'clock in the morning I started the 3-kilometer run. The passes were at 200 feet above the course and all the turns had to be made at low altitude and high speed. Back and forth I went over the 3-kilometer course four times, having the greatest difficulty in holding the plane on course in level flight due to a wing roll tendency at top speed, aided and abetted by turbulence.

I had made the record and landed, only to learn that the timing equipment had broken down.

So up the next morning I went for another try. I made two passes, under very trying conditions, and when it was evident that I could not better the mark, I aborted the flight and returned to base. I did not want a women's record, which I could easily have had, mixed in with the men's records I was after.

The plane was immediately refueled and the timing devices were shifted to the 15-kilometer course. The average of any two consecutive passes could be taken. The first pass was at a speed of 680 miles per hour. The second pass, with the wind against me, was at a speed of 670 miles per hour. I determined to make a third pass, even though the plane had developed a bad left-wing down roll at high speed and was in consequence next to unmanageable. On this third pass I decided to take a long dive at the conclusion of which I would level out before reaching the approach to the course. I did this but, on leveling out, the controls "froze" on me with the plane determined to roll over to the left.

I used both arms to pull on the controls and one knee as well for leverage but with no effect. Another second or two and the plane would have been over on its back and into the ground. I prevented this only by slowing it down. The timing camera did not catch me on that third pass.

I made the long turn for a landing and Chuck Yeager, in his chase plane, closed in behind me. He instructed me to leave the throttle untouched as much as possible and to land on the [dry] lake bed. I wanted to put the plane down on the runway where the ground crew was waiting but Chuck insisted that I put it down on the lake bed where I could take a high-speed landing and long roll.

I took off my oxygen mask and smelled fuel in the cockpit. When the wheels touched ground and the roll had about stopped, Chuck told me to cut the throttle and switches and get out as quickly as possible because I had a bad fuel leak which he had seen from his plane. A stream of fuel about the size of one's thumb was gushing out of the bottom of the main section of the left wing.

Passing the sonic barrier to beat the speed of sound was a

spiritual and emotional experience for me more than a physical one. Chuck Yeager was the first person to go through the barrier and live to tell about it. He acted as my mentor. No one else was to know about the plan. Time enough to talk about it when it was over because dozens of experienced and accomplished pilots had tried—some many times—to dive through that zone of shock waves and had failed.

On my first flight in the Canadian Sabre-jet I took it up to 30,000 feet and by putting it into a gentle dive I registered .97 of Mach 1. The next day I went to .99 of Mach 1. There was nothing left for me to do now on the third flight in that Sabre-jet except to pass Mach 1.

I climbed to about 45,000 feet. Then I did a "split S" to start the full-power and almost vertical dive and headed straight down for the airport. I counted aloud the changing readings on the Mach meter so Chuck could hear them. Mach .97, Mach .98, Mach .99, Mach 1, Mach 1.01.

At Mach .98 the wing suddenly dipped. Then it overcorrected and the right wing dipped. Then the nose tried to tuck under which means that the plane wanted to fly on its back. The turbulence was great and the shock waves violent.

Then I started to pull out of the dive gently so as to level off before getting below 18,000 feet altitude. Down there, in that heavy air, a pull-out might tear the plane apart.

I landed with one more barrier behind me and was much pleased. As my friends congratulated me I felt as if I were walking about ten feet above the ground. The men on the flight line heard the two explosions but they had not been recorded in the control tower. What should be done about that? The answer was easy. I would do it all over again.

So, at the end of an hour, I went up once more, only this time I wanted to do a little better so I climbed to 46,000 feet.

This time I stayed with the dive until I registered well above Mach 1 on the plane's Mach meter. This time the tower reported it, recorded the explosions and heard me counting the progress of the needle on the Mach meter. So I was highly satisfied.

Twice past the sonic barrier should have satisfied me, but Paramount Pictures and *Life* magazine had gotten wind of my proposed record speed flights and wanted their cameramen to be present. Finally I agreed, after talking to Chuck, that Chuck as the first man to go past the barrier and I as the first woman would do it together for them in separate planes flying a sort of supersonic duet.

We went to 48,000 feet this time and I put the Canadian Sabre-jet plane well above Mach 1 to give right good explosions. Incidentally this climb established a new women's international altitude record.

I am often asked what my sensations were while passing the barrier. There was no fear. There was confidence. And there was a great alertness to what was happening to the plane and what had to be done about it. At sonic speed it takes less than a minute to reach the ground from the start of the vertical power dive.

And there was another feeling—one of humility and trust. Way up there, about ten miles above the earth's surface, things come into proportion. The people on the ground have disappeared. You have left them behind and are on your own and impressed with the immensity of space and the divine order of things, which makes you realize with a feeling of comfort that you are not alone, that God is everywhere working in many ways His wonders to perform. That was why I had no fear and had confidence.

125

14. Charles E. Yeager
on Flying Faster
than Mach 1 and Mach 2

In 1943 the idea was conceived to design and build an airplane that would actually fly at speeds of Mach 1, the speed of sound, or a little faster.

The airplane went the way of all airplanes: drawing up on paper, trying, and improving and finally came out in 1946 in flyable condition. It was decided that this airplane, the X-1, should be powered with rocket power.

They thought maybe we had better drop this airplane from a B-29 because it carried only 288 gallons of liquid oxygen and 300 gallons of alcohol and this gave us enough fuel for only two and a half minutes of full power.

We went out to Edwards Air Force Base, California, where we had the large dry lake bed that at the time was seven miles long and five miles wide, which we figured we could hit on any dead-stick landing we had to make.

I could practically name who made what rivet, where. It is

very important when you are flying research airplanes like that, that you know your job. A lot of people are not with us anymore because of a little bit of haste when they do that sort of work.

On none of our takeoffs with the X-1 under the B-29 did we take off with the pilot in the X-1 cockpit, because if you had an inadvertent failure or had a fire and wanted to get rid of the X-1 you would probably lose the X-1 pilot too because he would not be high enough to recover from stall and spin. (The B-29's climbing speed was 180 miles per hour and the loaded X-1 had to be moving faster than 240 miles per hour, its stall speed, to successfully fly.)

So at 7000 feet above the ground you would climb down on a ladder which they would lower into the slipstream. You had your parachute on, of course. You would slide into the

Chuck Yeager with the X-1. (*U.S. Air Force*)

cockpit of the X-1 and get all squared around, they would slide the door down and you would hook it on from the inside, and then you would get your helmet on and get all connected up with your oxygen and radio and check in with the B-29 pilot.

On the initial flight of the X-1 that I made in August 1947, we flew the airplane without liquid oxygen or alcohol in it. We just took it up and dropped it to familiarize the pilot with the landing and stalling characteristics.

The first drop was quite an experience for me. You are sitting there. It is quite dark. The bomber pilot says: "I'll give you a five-minute warning here, and you can set up all your knobs the way they are supposed to be set up and set in and get a death grip on the stick." He gives you about a minute warning and then he starts counting down to five seconds and he says five seconds, four, three, two, one, drop, and the copilot finally releases you.

When you fall out, it comes out with a snap, and the bright sunlight usually blinds you quite severely for a matter of two or three seconds until you become acclimatized to the light. On the first flight, of course, it was just the same as a glider.

The motor consisted of four rocket tubes in the back, all tied together. You had four switches in the cockpit that you could turn on and off, start and stop a tube as many times as you wanted to, or until you ran out of fuel, of course.

My first powered flight, I wanted to feel out the engine. You turn on one chamber and you get a kick in the rear, and since your thrust is instantaneous there is no build-up. I tried out all four chambers by turning one chamber on and letting it run a few seconds and turning it off. Then I turned on three chambers, climbed up to 40,000 feet, accelerated up to 0.87 Mach number, or 87 percent of the speed of sound, shut

X-1 in flight. (*U.S. Air Force*)

everything off, jettisoned the remainder of the liquid oxygen and fuel, glided down, and landed.

We took small steps, increased our speed in very small increments, analyzed our data, and set up the next flight plan of exactly what we wanted to do. We had a camera mounted over the pilot's shoulder which started running at drop and ran until you landed. Besides the camera, we had recording instruments in the back. Besides that we carried either a 15- or 20-channel telemetering device which transmitted data to the ground.

On the second flight we took the airplane up to about 0.89 Mach number and we began to run into a little buffeting, the same as occurred with the old Mustangs or Spitfires or other airplanes at about 0.8 Mach.

A shock wave was forming at the thickest part of the wing and was starting to move back, and behind the shock wave you have turbulent air. This shock wave also killed off a little more lift on one wing than it did on the other one, so you would get a slight wing drop. It is almost impossible to make one wing a perfect replica of the other one.

On about the fourth flight we took the airplane up to 0.94 Mach number, 94 percent of the speed of sound. At this speed I pulled on the control column and the airplane did not turn, it went the way it was headed. So I shut everything off and came down and had a heart to heart talk with the engineers.

We looked at all our data and it showed that the shock wave that had formed on the horizontal stabilizers, the same as on the wing, had moved back and attached itself to the trailing edge of the stabilizer just in front of where the elevator was hinged.

Finally they came out with the next program. Instead of turning with the elevator—the flippers on the airplane—we would change the angle of the whole tail and make the airplane turn.

After that it was just a matter of a couple of flights. The buffeting got very heavy and we did get a little bit of pitch up. We kicked it on up on the sixth flight to about 1.04 Mach number. This was the first flight faster than sound—October 14, 1947.

They came out with another airplane: the X-1A. It was practically a duplication of the X-1 No. 3. I was assigned as the project pilot.

Since December 17, 1953, was to be the 50th anniversary of powered flight, all of our powers-that-be said it would be real nice if we could get up to above Mach 2 (twice the speed of sound) before the 50th Anniversary.

The engineers got together and figured out the flight plan: dropping out at 30,000 feet, lighting off three of the four chambers, accelerating up to 0.8 Mach number, climbing at 0.8 Mach number to 45,000 feet, firing the fourth chamber, leveling out, accelerating up to 1.1, and then going through a climb schedule up to a certain altitude and leveling off and letting the airplane run till it ran out of fuel.

On the first flight, they dropped me at 30,000 feet and I fired off three chambers, went up to 45,000 feet, fired off the fourth one, and the airplane reacted exactly in the same way as the old X-1. After you get up to about 1.1 your airplane smooths out, your buffeting drops away, your airplane trims up again, the wing will rise—the one it dropped—and you can get the elevator control back again.

The second flight, I took it up to 50,000 feet, let it sit till it got up to 1.5, shut it off, and jettisoned the remainder of the liquid oxygen and fuel, and came down and landed. We looked at our data and I pretty well had the flight plan down perfect, which was important.

The third flight, I leveled out at around 60,000 feet, held it straight and level, and ran it up to 1.9 Mach number, which is about 1200 mph, shut it off, and came down and landed.

The fourth and last flight actually was on December 12th; we beat our schedule a little. We dropped the airplane out at 30,000 feet. At 45,000 feet we had all four chambers going.

We went up to about 1.1 Mach number and started climbing. We went through 50,000 feet at about 1.15 and went through 60,000 feet at about 1.4.

I was supposed to start leveling out at 61,000 or 62,000 feet, but due to the excited nature of the pilot I overshot. Actually, I got to around 68,000 feet before I started pushing over, came level at 78,000 feet, and was indicating about 1.9 Mach number. I held it there straight and level. The airplane ran out of fuel at about 76,000 feet and at a Mach number of a little better than 2.5.

We overstepped our bounds a little bit. When I ran out of fuel, the airplane started decelerating. At that point we lost all stability. The airplane started more or less changing ends, so we had a moment of anxiety there.

The airplane got some pretty high rates of roll and yaw and pitch angles. The airplane started rolling to the right to start with, so I put all the controls against the rolls, as they taught me in flying school, and it did not help. So I put them with it, and it did not help. I let them loose and started praying.

The airplane was going 1650 mph at about 76,000 feet and, 51 seconds later, settled at 25,000 feet and 170 mph, so I had not much time.

I was pretty well blacked out due to the high acceleration forces.

I rolled the stabilizer in but overshot, and the airplane got into an inverted spin, so I came back to neutral, put everything with the inverted spin, flipped into a normal spin, and I recovered at 25,000 feet and glided on back to the lake.

That was the last flight I made in the airplane.

15. Alan B. Shepard, Jr., First American into Space

I honestly never felt that I would be the first man to ride the Mercury capsule. After my name was read off I did not say anything for about 20 seconds or so. I just looked at the floor. When I looked up, everyone in the room was staring at me. I thanked Mr. [Robert] Gilruth for his confidence. Then the others, with grins on their faces covering up what must have been their own great disappointment, came over and congratulated me.

I stuck close to the capsule as the workmen put it together, piece by piece, and then hung around to watch as the engineers tested it, section by section. I was more familiar with that capsule when it was all over than I have ever been with any other piece of hardware in my life.

On the morning of [Tuesday] May 2, 1961, when I was first scheduled to go, a heavy rain was falling outside and flashes of lightning were playing around the launching pad.

Thursday morning we got pretty fair weather reports. I

went to bed at ten. I went off to sleep in 10 or 15 minutes. There were no dreams or nightmares or charging around on the bed. I woke up once, about midnight, and went to the window to check on the stars. I could see them, so I went back to sleep.

A little after 1 A.M. I got up, shaved and showered and had breakfast with John Glenn and Bill Douglas. There were butterflies in my stomach again, but I did not feel that I was coming apart or that things were getting ahead of me. A little after four, we left the hangar and got started for the pad.

I sort of wanted to kick the tires—the way you do with a new car or an airplane. I realized that I would probably never see that missile again. It's a lovely sight. The Redstone with the Mercury capsule and escape tower on top of it is a particularly good-looking combination, long and slender. And this one had a decided air of expectancy about it. It stood there full of lox [liquid oxygen], venting white clouds and rolling frost down the side.

At 5:20 I squeezed through the hatch. I linked the suit up with the capsule oxygen system, checked the straps which held me tight in the couch, and removed the safety pins which kept some of the switches from being pushed or pulled inadvertently.

At 6:10, the hatch went on and I was alone.

I went through all the check-off lists, checked the radio systems and the gyro switches. On the big map inside Mercury Control, which showed the locations and status of the tracking stations, recovery ships and communications net, all the lights were green. All conditions were "Go." The gantry rolled back at 6:34, and I lay on my back 70 feet above the ground checking the straps and switches and waiting for the countdown to proceed.

[Deke Slayton] read the final count. "Ten, nine, eight, seven . . ." At the count of 5, I put my right hand on the stopwatch button, which I had to push at liftoff to time the flight. I put my left hand on the abort handle, which I would move in a hurry only if something went seriously wrong and I had to activate the escape tower.

Just after the count of zero, Deke said, "Liftoff." Then he added a final tension-breaker to make me relax.

"You're on your way, José," he said.

I think I braced myself a bit too much while Deke was giving me the final count. Nobody knew, of course, how much shock and vibration I would really feel when I took off. There was no one around who had tried it and could tell me.

There was a lot less vibration and noise rumble than I had expected. It was extremely smooth—a subtle, gentle, gradual rise off the ground. There was nothing rough or abrupt about it. But there was no question that I was going, either. I could see it on the instruments, hear it on the headphones, feel it all around me.

It was no good for them to have a test pilot up there unless they knew fairly precisely what he was doing, what he saw and how he felt every 30 seconds or so along the way. I was scheduled to communicate about something or other for a total of 78 times during the 15 minutes that I was up. And I had to manage or at least monitor a total of 27 major events in the capsule. This kept me rather busy.

One minute after liftoff the ride did get a little rough. This was where the booster and the capsule passed from sonic to supersonic speed and then immediately went slicing through a zone of maximum dynamic pressure as the forces of speed and air density combined at their peak.

The spacecraft started vibrating here. Although my vision

was blurred for a few seconds, I had no trouble seeing the instrument panel. I decided not to report this sensation just then. I did not want to panic anyone into ordering me to leave. And I did not *want* to leave. So I waited until the vibration stopped and let the Control Center know indirectly by reporting to Deke that it was "a lot smoother now, a lot smoother."

At two minutes after launch, at an altitude of about 22 miles, the Gs were building up and I was climbing at a speed of 3200 miles per hour. The ride was fine now, and I made my last transmission before the booster engine cut off: ". . . All systems are 'Go.' "

The engine cutoff occurred right on schedule, at two minutes and 22 seconds after liftoff. Nothing abrupt happened, just a delicate and gradual dropping off of the thrust as the fuel flow decreased.

I heard a noise as the little rockets fired to separate the capsule from the booster. This was a critical point of the flight, both technically and psychologically. I knew that if the capsule got hung up on the booster, I would have quite a different flight.

Right after leaving the booster, the capsule and I went weightless together and I could feel the capsule begin its slow, lazy turnaround to get into position for the rest of the flight. It turned 180 degrees, with the blunt or bottom end swinging forward now to take up the heat.

The periscope went out at this point, and I was supposed to do three things in order: (1) take over manual control of the capsule; (2) tell the people downstairs how the controls were working; and (3) take a look outside to see what the view was like.

The capsule was traveling at about 5000 miles per hour now, and up to this point it had been on automatic pilot. I switched over to the manual control stick, and tried out the pitch, yaw, and roll axes in that order. Each time I moved the stick, the little jets of hydrogen peroxide rushed through the nozzles on the outside of the capsule and pushed it or twisted it the way I wanted it to go. This was a big moment for me, for it proved that our control system was sound and that it worked under real space-flight conditions.

No one could be briefed well enough to be completely prepared for the astonishing view that I got. My exclamation back to Deke about the "beautiful sight" was completely spontaneous. It was breathtaking. To the south I could see where the cloud cover stopped at about Fort Lauderdale, and that the weather was clear all the way down past the Florida Keys. To the north I could see up the coast of the Carolinas to where the clouds just obscured Cape Hatteras.

All through this period, the capsule and I remained weightless. The sensation was just what I expected it would be: pleasant and relaxing. It had absolutely no effect on my movements or my efficiency. The ends of my straps floated around a little, and there was some dust drifting around in the cockpit with me. But these were unimportant.

About 115 miles up—very near the apogee of my flight—Deke Slayton started to give me the countdown for the retrofiring maneuver. This had nothing directly to do with my flight from a technical standpoint. I was established on a ballistic path and there was nothing the retro-rockets could do to sway me from it. But we would be using these rockets as brakes on the big orbital flights to start the capsule back toward earth. We wanted to try them on the trip just to see how well they worked. We also wanted to test *my* reactions to them and check on the pilot's ability to keep the capsule under control as they went off.

At five minutes and 14 seconds after launch, the first of the three rockets went off, right on schedule. The other two went off at the prescribed five-second intervals. There was a small upsetting motion as our speed was reduced, and I was pushed back into the couch a bit by the sudden change in Gs. But each time the capsule started to get pushed out of its proper angle

Alan B. Shepard, Jr., rides helicopter sling after ocean landing. (*NASA*)

by one of the retros going off I found that I could bring it back again with no trouble at all. I was able to stay on top of the flight by using the manual controls, and this was perhaps the most encouraging product of the entire mission.

We were on our way down now and I waited for the package which holds the retro-rockets on the bottom of the capsule to jettison and get out of the way. It blew off on schedule. The green light which was supposed to report this event failed to light up on the instrument panel. This was our only signal failure of the mission. I pushed an override button, however, and the light turned green as it was supposed to do. This meant that everything was all right.

The pressure of the air we were coming into began to overcome the force of the control jets, and it was no longer possible to make the capsule respond.

In that long plunge back to earth, I was pushed back into the couch with a force of about 11 Gs. All the way down, as the altimeter spun through mile after mile of descent, I kept grunting out "O.K., O.K., O.K.," just to show them back in the Control Center how I was doing.

The temperature climbed to 1230 degrees Fahrenheit on the outer walls. But it never went above 100 degrees in the cabin or above 82 degrees in my suit. I knew from talking to Deke that my trajectory looked good and that *Freedom 7* was going to land right in the center of the recovery area.

Looking through the periscope, I could see the antenna canister blow free on top of the capsule. The canister, in turn, pulled out the bag which held the main chute and pulled *it* free. And then, all of a sudden, there it was—the main chute stretching out long and thin. Four seconds later the huge orange and white canopy blossomed out above me.

About 1000 feet I looked out through the porthole and saw

Shepard and capsule on carrier after splashdown. (*NASA*)

the water coming up toward me. I braced myself in the couch for the impact, but it was not at all bad. It was a little abrupt, but no more severe than the jolt a Navy pilot gets when he is launched off the catapult of a carrier.

The spacecraft hit and then it flopped over on its side so that I was leaning over on my right side in the couch. I hit the switch to kick the reserve parachute loose. This would take some of the weight off the top of the capsule and help it right itself.

I could not see any water seeping into the capsule, but I could hear all kinds of gurgling sounds around me, so I was not sure whether we were leaking or not. I had just started to make a final reading on all of the instruments when the helicopter pilot called me. I had told him I was in good shape, but he seemed in a hurry to get me out.

"O.K.," he said, "you've got two minutes to come out."

I decided he knew what he was doing and that following his instructions was perhaps more important than taking those extra readings. I opened the door and crawled to a sitting position on the sill. The pilot lowered the horse-collar sling; I grabbed it, slipped it on, and then began the slow ride up into the helicopter.

When we approached the ship, I could see sailors crowding the deck, applauding and cheering and waving their caps. I felt a real lump in my throat.

16. Joseph A. Walker
on Flying Above the Atmosphere

The time had come. I said, "Launch now!" and flicked a switch, releasing the shackles that held the X-15 beneath the wing of the B-52 mother plane cruising at 45,500 feet.

For a split second we fell like a bomb, my black bird and I. Then I had her under control in a fast glide toward the glaring rock and sand of the Nevada desert.

More than 1400 feet below the B-52 we "got a light," or engine start, and the X-15's liquid rocket cut in with explosive force. Under full throttle it began a rapid build-up to the power of 548,000 raging horses, more than twice the horse-power of the biggest United States Navy carrier.

"And I'm on my way!" I said.

My radioed comment must have sounded as exultant as I felt. If all went well, I would pilot the research X-15, half plane, half missile, to its design altitude of 250,000 feet, or 47.3 miles above the earth. I was shooting for a new record.

The record, however, was incidental. My main purpose: to explore speeds faster than a high-powered bullet and the problems of controlled re-entry into the atmosphere.

Acceleration from that inferno in the tail pipe pinned me back in my seat with a force of 2 Gs, twice the force of gravity,

Joseph A. Walker in the X-15. (*U.S. Air Force*)

X-15 launches from B-52 mother plane's wing. (*NASA*)

hence twice my weight of 164 pounds. Pulling back on the control stick, I increased my climb angle to 38°.

Three Gs . . . 4 Gs . . . the force built up rapidly. I felt as though I were flat on. my back and climbing vertically. My bullet would have to be slowed a bit to follow the carefully planned flight path. Right on schedule, after 40 seconds of powered flight, I popped out the speed brakes.

Ground control at Edwards began tolling a countdown for engine shutoff. We had planned on 81 seconds of engine burning time—and that meant 81 on the nose, not 83 or 84. A few extra seconds would propel me far above the intended altitude and stretch the arc of my flight. Coming back for a dead-stick landing, I might find myself beyond gliding range of the hard, dry floor of Rogers Lake at Edwards [AFB, California]. That could be a fatal embarrassment.

Call-outs from the ground had grown weak; now they faded away. No matter. I had checked my own countdown clock with the first call-outs; it was accurate.

At 79 seconds I reached for the throttle with my left hand —and grasped nothing. Glancing down quickly, I saw my gloved fingers were a good two inches from the handle. G-forces had plastered me so far back in the seat that I couldn't reach it.

But I *had* to. Bracing against right elbow and shoulder, I lunged forward with all my strength. That did it. I got the throttle off a second late—at 81.6 seconds, to be precise.

It's strange how many thoughts I compressed into those fleeting moments. The unwanted altitude flashed through my mind. I envisioned what would happen to me, decided on what to do, and did it.

All five of the present X-15 pilots have experienced similar compression of thought during critical moments. We are consistently able to recall things that occurred in split seconds as though they extended over longer periods of time. We seem to undergo a time dilation, perhaps due to the adrenalin coursing through our systems.

Engine shutdown came at 3443 miles an hour—nearly five times the speed of sound—and an altitude of 142,800 feet. I was weightless immediately, and it felt pleasant, a welcome relief. The ends of checklist pages on my clipboard rose eerily, and a little cloud of dirt particles drifted up from the floor. Sunlight lanced through the left windshield at these motes; I could even see that they were of different sizes and shapes.

Upward the X-15 soared in coasting flight. In effect, it had become a cannon shell in space; it followed a fixed arc, just as a shell does, in response to the inexorable laws of physics. Once the X-15 is outside the atmosphere, its flight path, or arc, cannot be changed without engine power. I could not alter my course until I fell back into the air and regained aerodynamic control.

But I could change my craft's attitude. I could dip the wings and move the nose up and down or from side to side. Yes, I could even have turned around and climbed tail first, though that would have been foolish.

For movements in space the X-15 has small jet controls, like the Mercury capsules. Hydrogen peroxide, forced over a catalyst of silver, breaks down into steam and oxygen and spurts from little openings in the nose and wings. A control stick on the left side of the cockpit operates these jets. You need them to keep the plane from twisting and tumbling and to put it into the right attitude for re-entry.

I used the jets immediately after engine cutoff. My lunge for the throttle had made the nose bob down, so I blasted it up and smoothed out other small movements. The reaction controls felt fine, and I tried a 30° left bank angle, then rolled level and pointed the nose back on the correct heading.

Seconds later we coasted up to the peak of our arc. My instruments showed exactly 250,000 feet. These are special instruments, part of an inertial data system. Its heart is a little platform, kept stable by gyroscopes, that always points to the earth's center. On the platform are instruments that sense changes in acceleration, hence changes in speed and direction. A computer in the airplane remembers these changes and disgorges data on course, attitude, speed, and height.

X-15 pilots complain that there isn't any time for sightseeing, but we always take a quick look around from the top of the hill. On my left I saw the Gulf of California and looked down the peninsula of Baja California to a cloud mass smothering its tip. On my right I glimpsed Monterey Bay. Way out in front, and as far around as I could see, the horizon curved like a scimitar.

A bright band of light, not as sharply defined as I had remembered it from an earlier flight, hugged the horizon. Above it the sky shaded into a magnificent deep violet. Below me the ground returned strong sunlight with brilliant sparkles.

As we coasted over the hump and the nose tipped down, I could see the white glare of Rogers Lake, with its 12-mile length of sunbaked clay, right where it was supposed to be. As always, I felt regret in leaving space and returning to that old cumbersome gravity.

But now I had to think about the most critical part of the flight, re-entry. You have to do this maneuver right, or buddy, you "bought the farm," pilots' jargon for a fast retirement. If I had slashed into the atmosphere with the nose straight down, G-forces on the pull-out would have broken up the X-15. What's more, she couldn't have survived the heat. Her skin, of Inconel "X," a nickel-chromium alloy, will withstand 1200° Fahrenheit, but the heat load on a straight dive would have been far too great. There was also a third consideration. If I had dived straight down, I wouldn't have had enough room for a safe pull-out and landing.

So, using the jet controls, I pushed the nose to an 18° angle of attack and plunged "belly buster" into the atmosphere. In this position part of the underside of the X-15 helped brake my fall.

My speed, about 3000 miles an hour at re-entry, was so great that I could have picked up a little aerodynamic control at about 150,000 feet. But I had some pronounced side-to-side movement to worry about, and I stayed with the jets. At

100,000 feet the G-forces began mounting rapidly, soon reaching 5½ Gs, and I could feel bladders in my suit puffing up to grip me tightly and dam the downward flow of blood.

As the Gs built up, so did the heat. It reached a peak of 1000° F., recorded on the speed brakes. Leading edges of wings, nose, and tail soaked up enough heat to glow a dull red.

Below 100,000 feet I no longer needed the jets, and at 65,000 feet the X-15 pulled out in gliding flight. My comment to the ground: "I sure felt that one!" The dry lake lay about 35 miles away, and I had plenty of altitude to fly a lazy approach.

I touched the X-15's steel skids down at more than 200 miles an hour on the baked clay of the dry lake. The nose wheel came down hard—whomp!—and we slid a mile and a quarter.

"Well, there's that one for today," I said to ground control.

But the mild exuberance I always feel after a good flight was soon marred. Radar readings said my altitude instruments lied. Two radar stations placed my maximum height at 246,700 feet, or 46.7 miles, a little short of the intended goal. Apparently the engine didn't give quite the expected thrust.

Even so, the [April 30, 1962] flight set a record.

17. Virgil Grissom on Spacecraft Maneuvers

John [Young] and I went methodically on with our checks, the voices from the blockhouse keeping us abreast on the countdown.

"T minus zero! Stage One ignition!"

There was a distant, muffled thunder 90 feet below our heavily insulated cabin. This was the split second during which our Malfunction Detection System had to warn me if something had gone wrong, and I had both hands on the ejection ring between my knees, ready to yank it hard if the MDS indicators on our instrument panels indicated we were in trouble.

Three seconds later, liftoff! We were on our way [March 23, 1965].

Our launch sequence had gone perfectly, with booster and sustaining engine cut-outs taking place precisely as scheduled. Shortly after liftoff, though, our onboard computer had told

John W. Young and Virgil I. Grissom. (*NASA*)

us we were going higher on the flight path than expected. Our booster was just a little bit "hot."

But now we were in earth orbit, with an 87-mile perigee and a 125-mile apogee, just about as planned, and then, as we passed beyond the Canary Islands . . .

First, John told me that the pressure in the oxygen system, which kept us alive, had suddenly dropped both in our suits and in the spacecraft. Then I spotted some bad readings in other places. Reacting automatically, I yanked my visor down and then it struck me: "If the oxygen pressure is really gone, it won't make any difference. You've had it already."

Actually, as it turned out, we had plenty of oxygen. We just didn't have the right readings. An electrical converter system which powered our instruments had malfunctioned.

John was smarter than I was. Figuring he wasn't suffocating yet, he reached up and switched on a back-up converter.

Now I had to do one of the scientific experiments. All I had

Grissom and Young in *Gemini* trainer. (*NASA*)

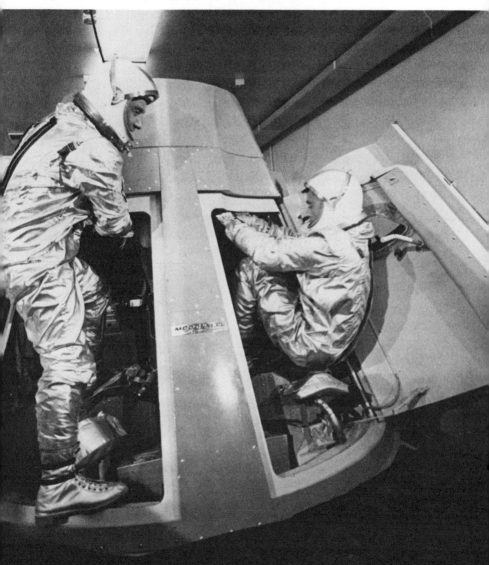

to do was turn a knob, but I twisted that handle so hard I broke it off.

About this time John was supposed to check out some of our space meals. I was concentrating on our spacecraft's performance, when suddenly John asked me, "You care for a corned beef sandwich, skipper?"

If I could have fallen out of my couch, I would have. Sure enough, he was holding out an honest-to-john corned beef sandwich. He'd had the sandwich made up at a Cocoa Beach restaurant and tucked it into one of the pockets of his space suit. I thanked John and took a bite, but crumbs of rye bread started floating around the cabin, and it became instantly obvious that our life-support system wasn't prepared to cope with the high-powered aroma. Reluctantly, I stowed it away.

We were [fascinated] by the chance to carry out some real space "firsts," changing our orbit and nudging our spacecraft from one flight path to another, or "changing plane." To our intense satisfaction we were able to carry out these maneuvers almost exactly as planned, confirming that our *Gemini* spacecraft was capable of rendezvous missions, in which changes of orbit and flight path are a requirement. To the best of our knowledge no astronaut or spacecraft had ever accomplished these maneuvers before.

The longer we flew, the more jubilant we felt. We had a really fine spacecraft, one we could be proud of in every respect.

Almost before we could believe it, it was time to prepare for the most critical part of our flight, retro-fire and re-entry. This is when you know the whole world is watching you, holding its breath, and giving a sigh of relief along with you when those retro-rockets fire.

What a comfortable feeling as our couches slammed our

backs, as each of the retro-rockets ignited and we began to sense the G-forces of re-entry.

Then our onboard computer told us we would land far short of our recovery carrier, the *Intrepid.* And here we were able to bring off another first, by performing two banking maneuvers during the re-entry phase to give us maximum lift. This reduced the error considerably and allowed us to land only 58 miles short of the predicted landing point.

The one real surprise to me was the jolt we both got when our main chute deployed. John and I were both thrown against our windows, and I banged into a knob that punctured my face plate. John's face plate was scratched. And then we were in the water.

The flight of *Gemini 3* had taken four hours and fifty-three minutes. John and I had been around the world three times.

18. Michael Collins
on Walking in Space

As dawn arrives [July 20, 1966], I am precisely on schedule and ready to go.

"Mike's going outside right now."

My first job is to get back behind the cockpit next to Thruster 16, where the nitrogen valve is and where a micrometeorite detection plate has been exposed for the past two days. I remove the plate with no difficulty, making sure that John [Young] doesn't fire 16 while my hand is practically crammed down its nozzle.

"Watch that thruster there, babe . . . I'm by it."

"O.K.," John replies.

I am facing the side of the *Gemini* with my feet lazily swinging back and forth as I try to make my way along a handrail with the micrometeorite plate in one hand. I guess I'm far enough away from 16 now. Or am I?

"Wait! O.K., go ahead."

I now manage to reach the cockpit, hand the plate in to John through the open hatch, and then start back to connect my gun to its nitrogen supply.

John gets a new idea. "Hey! Can we back out a little?"

I don't care about those thrusters. I'm not near them. "Yes, go ahead."

My problem is that there are two handrails, one raised manually by me, and the other, which is supposed to pop up automatically. I have raised the former prior to retrieving the micrometeorite plate, but the latter has only popped up at one end, the end farthest away from the cockpit, and the near end is still almost flush with the skin of the *Gemini.* My plan calls for winding my nitrogen line under the handrail and then connecting it to the nitrogen valve, but clearly there is not enough room to get the bulky nitrogen connector under the flattened rail, despite a couple of good healthy tugs.

Finally, I decide to make the connection without the loop under the rail. I remove the cover plate from the nitrogen valve, get positioned as best I can, using the two handrails to torque my body into place directly above the valve; and then holding a rail in my right hand and the connector in my left, I ram the connector down onto its mate.

Missed.

The sleeve on the connector has sprung forward and must be recocked (a two-handed operation). In the meantime, the reaction to my shove has caused my body to lurch over to one side, and my legs bang up against the side of the spacecraft. John feels the commotion and so does the *Gemini's* control system, which resents the unwanted swaying motion I am creating and fires thrusters to restore itself to an even keel.

I am now poised for another stab at the nitrogen connector. When my body is in the right position once again, I quietly

John W. Young and Michael Collins. (*NASA*)

release both hands and—floating free for a second—reach down and recock the connector, find the handrail again, and give the connection another shove.

Made it! "O.K., I'm hooked into the nitrogen."

"O.K.," says John.

Now we have to contend with the floating loop in the nitrogen line, which is the result of my having hooked it up without first detouring it around under the handrail. If the slack is not taken up, it will assuredly drift over on top of good old Thruster 16 and get severed just when I need it.

"I'm coming back into the cockpit area for just a second here . . . See that loose nitrogen line? You're going to have to snub that down some place. Can you do that?"

"Where is it?"

I dangle it down inside the open right hatch. "See it?"

"Yes."

"Got it?"

"Yes." I don't know what he's going to do with it, sit on it if necessary, but he's in a better position to cope with it than I.

Gently, gently, I push away from *Gemini*, hopefully balancing the pressure of my right hand on the open hatch with that of my left hand on the spacecraft itself. As I float out of the cockpit, upward and slightly forward, I note with relief that I am not snagged on anything but am traveling in a straight line with no tendency to pitch or yaw as I go.

It's not more than three or four seconds before I collide with my target, the docking adapter on the end of the *Agena*. A cone-shaped affair with a smooth edge, it is a lousy spot to land, because there are no ready handholds, but this is the end where the micrometeorite package is located and, after all, that is what I have come so far to retrieve.

I grab the slippery lip of the docking cone with both hands and start working my way around it. As I move I dislodge part of the docking apparatus, an electric discharge ring which springs loose, dangling from one attaching point. It looks like a thin scythe with a wicked hook, two feet in diameter. Best I stay clear of it.

By this time, I have reached the package, and now I must

stop. [But] I am falling off! I have built up too much momentum, and now the inertia in my torso and legs keeps me moving; first my right hand, and then my left, feel the *Agena* slither away, despite my desperate clutch. As I slowly cartwheel away from the *Agena,* I see absolutely nothing but black sky for several seconds, and then the *Gemini* hoves into view.

Where I am slowly comes into view and perspective. I am up above the *Gemini* about 15 or 20 feet, in front of it and looking down at John's window and my own open hatch. The *Agena* is below me to my left, and slightly behind me. My motion is taking me away from the *Agena,* but it is tangential relative to the *Gemini,* which is not pleasant, because the laws of physics tell me that as I get closer to it (as my radius decreases), my velocity will increase and I may splat up against it at a nasty rate of speed.

Fortunately, I have my gun, my maneuvering unit, stuck on my hip. It can null, or at least reduce, my tangential velocity so that I can safely make it back to the *Gemini.* I reach for it. It's gone!

I grope until I find the hose leading to it, and discover the gun isn't really gone, it's just trailing out behind me. I reel in the hose, open the arms of the gun, and start hosing. I am squirting nitrogen out through two tiny nozzles pointed in a direction I have selected to (1) reduce my tangential velocity, (2) increase my radial velocity toward the *Gemini,* and (3) keep me pointed toward the *Gemini.*

The gun is not capable of changing this path entirely, but it does modify it enough so that I come sailing around in a slow arc and straighten out as I fly behind the *Gemini,* a location I have never intended to explore.

"I'm back behind the cockpit, John, so don't fire any thrusters."

"O.K., we have to go down, if we want to stay with it [the *Agena*]."

"Don't go down right now. *John, do not go down.* " If he does, it will not only fire thrusters near me, but, worse yet, it will cause my target to sink below me just at the moment I am having difficulty getting down to it.

"O.K.," he says.

Now things are getting better: I am approaching the cockpit from the rear. My approach isn't exactly graceful, and it's still a bit too swift for my liking, but as I reach the open hatch, I snag it with one arm and it slows me practically to a stop. It is now a simple matter to get the umbilical cord pulled in, and to stuff it and myself back inside the open hatch. Time for another try.

This time I decide to use my gun to translate over to the *Agena,* so John doesn't have to fly so close to it. When John gets us into position, I depart the cockpit by squirting my gun up, pointing it right at the end of the *Agena.* Up I glide, miraculously it seems, pulling myself up by my bootstraps.

As my left bootstrap reaches the top of the instrument panel, my foot snags on something briefly and causes me to start a gentle face-down pitching motion. Just as a diver wants to hit the water head first, not flat on his back, so do I wish not to splat into the *Agena* back first, so I have some quick adjustments to make with the gun. I hold it in the proper position to create an upward pitch, and after a few seconds of squirting in this direction, I have restored my desired orientation.

I now discover to my horror, however, that I am gently rising up and that my path is no longer taking me to the end of the *Agena* but just above it. Fortunately, I have just enough time to make one last frantic correction, and as I cruise by, I am able to reach my left arm down and snag the *Agena,* just

159

barely. As my body swings around, in response to this new torque, I am able to plunge my right hand down into the recess between the docking adapter and the main body of the *Agena,* and find some wires to cling to. I'm not going to slip off this time!

After all this, I have lost my bearings, and I don't know which way to move to find the meteorite package. Of course, since the end of the *Agena* is circular, I will wind up at the right spot eventually . . .

Finally, I make it around to the package. What a pleasant surprise when the two buttons stay depressed and the fairing jerks loose with only a moderate pull, bringing with it the package dangling by the two wires!

John is worried about my getting fouled with the *Agena,* which is starting to move now. I have yanked, pulled, and twisted the end of it on two occasions, and its response has by now become obvious to John. I can't see its motion, but I can feel that when I push against it, it seems less than rock-steady.

Gemini 10 returns to earth. Young in raft, Collins leaving capsule. (*NASA*)

John registers his alarm. "Come back . . . get out of all that garbage . . . just come on back, babe."

I have my package, and although I am supposed to replace the old micrometeorite experiment with a new one, it doesn't seem a wise move. The *Agena* is tumbling slowly.

"Don't worry. Don't worry. Here I come."

I am coming home the easy way, hand over hand on my umbilical, but *slowly,* to avoid going fast enough to splat up against the side of it when I get there.

I am now back at the open right hatch, and I make a very sad discovery. I have lost my camera, which I had stuck into a slot on the side of my chest pack.

[The] umbilical cord is wound around me at least a couple of times. John sees my predicament and is able to reach over far enough to unloop one coil. Now I have to back out, and John guides my feet and yanks a bit, and I am nearly free, with only one persistent loop around me.

I wedge my body down through the coils, forcing my legs deep into the footwell, jackknifing my knees until my torso swings down and inward in that old familiar motion I have practiced a hundred times in the zero-G airplane. I grab the hatch above me and swing it gingerly toward the closed position.

Click! Success!

19. Edwin E. Aldrin, Jr., on the First Moon Landing

We were still sixty miles above the surface of the backside of the moon when we made our first burn of 28.5 seconds to begin our coasting descent to the front side of the moon. Neil [Armstrong] and I were harnessed into the LM [Lunar Module] in a standing position.

At precisely the right moment the engine ignited to begin the 12-minute powered descent. Strapped in by the system of belts and cables not at all unlike shock absorbers, neither of us felt the initial motion. We looked quickly at the computer to make sure we were actually functioning as planned. After 26 seconds the engine went to full throttle and the motion became noticeable.

At 6000 feet above the lunar surface a yellow caution light came on and we encountered one of the few potentially serious problems in the entire flight, a problem which might have caused us to abort, had it not been for a man on the ground who really knew his job.

When the yellow program alarm light came on we routinely asked the computer to define its problem. The coded answer it gave was that the machine was overloaded; it was being asked to do too much in too little time.

Back in Houston, not to mention on board the *Eagle,* hearts shot up into throats while we waited to learn what would happen.

We had received two of the caution lights when Steven Bales, the flight controller responsible for LM computer activity, perceived the problem and told us to proceed. We received three or four more warnings but kept on going. When Mike [Collins], Neil, and I were presented with Medals of Freedom by President Nixon, Steve also received one. He certainly deserved it, because without him we might not have landed.

At an altitude of 500 feet, Neil took over manually, and together we began our final descent. We immediately saw that the area of the moon where our computer intended to land was rather more strewn with rocks than we had anticipated. The area beyond it, however, was quite clear. Neil extended our trajectory and thereby changed our touchdown point.

At an altitude of 50 feet we entered what was accurately referred to as the dead-man zone. In this zone, if anything had gone wrong—if, for example, the engine had failed—it would probably have been too late to do anything about it before we impacted with the moon. I felt no apprehension at all during this short time. Rather, I felt a kind of arrogance—an arrogance inspired by knowing that so many people had worked on this landing, people possessing the greatest scientific talents in the world.

We touched down on the lunar surface. The landing was so smooth I had to check the landing lights from the touchdown

Neil A. Armstrong, Michael Collins, Edwin E. Aldrin, Jr. (*NASA*)

sensors to make sure the slight bump I felt was indeed the landing. It was.

"Contact light. O.K., engine stopped," I communicated back to Houston, quickly launching into the post-engine procedures in preparation for the possibility of an immediate abort liftoff. We had trained to do exactly this and I was surprised when Neil interrupted to say, "Houston, Tranquility Base here. The *Eagle* has landed."

We gave in to our excitement long enough to pat each other on the shoulder, then we plunged into frantic activity. Before beginning preparations to go out onto the lunar surface we were planning for the first of several emergency liftoff times to rejoin the *Columbia.* The first came less than one minute after touchdown and was followed less than two minutes later by the second such ideal time for rendezvous.

The first two hours on the lunar surface were, for me, the busiest part of the flight. I had to make all sorts of measurements and alignments with stars for navigational purposes. This all had to be communicated back to earth and rechecked by voice—a process that is as long as it is boring to listen to.

According to the flight plan, this sequence was followed by an eating period and a four-hour rest period before we were scheduled to start the involved preparations to walk on the lunar surface. It was called a rest period, but it was also a built-in time pad in case we had to make an extra lunar orbit before landing, or if there was any kind of difficulty which might delay the landing. Since we landed on schedule and weren't overly tired, as we had thought we might be, we opted to skip the four-hour rest period. We were too excited to sleep anyway.

During the first idle moment in the LM before eating our snack, I pulled out two small packages which had been specially prepared at my request. One contained a small amount of wine, the other a small wafer. With them and a small chalice, I took communion on the moon.

It was very cramped in the *Eagle.* We felt like two fullbacks trying to change positions inside a Cub Scout pup tent. We also had to be careful of our movements. The LM structure was so thin one of us could have taken a pencil and jammed it through the side of the ship.

We opened the hatch, and Neil, with me as his navigator, began backing out of the tiny opening. We were so busy that neither of us noticed that Neil had momentarily forgotten to pull the small handle he passed on the small porch of the LM. The handle deploys the side of the LM where all the equipment we needed on the lunar surface was stored, and it also activated the television camera that was going to televise back to earth his step onto the lunar surface. The ground noticed the omission and reminded Neil, who moved back a bit and pulled the deployment handle.

It seemed like a small eternity before I heard Neil say, at 10:56 P.M., "That's one small step for man . . . ah . . . one giant leap for mankind." It was a neatly appropriate expression.

In less than 15 minutes I was backing awkwardly out of the hatch and onto the surface to join Neil, who, in the tradition of all tourists, had his camera ready to photograph my arrival.

I felt buoyant and was full of goose pimples when I stepped down on the surface.

I quickly discovered that I felt balanced—comfortably upright—only when I was tilted slightly forward. I also felt a bit disoriented: on the earth when one looks at the horizon, it appears flat; on the moon, so much smaller than the earth and quite without high terrain, the horizon in all directions visibly curved down away from us.

As we had planned, I took off jogging to test my maneuverability on the surface. The exercise gave me an odd sensation and looked even more odd when I later saw films of it. With the bulky suits on, we appeared to be moving in slow motion. I noticed immediately that my inertia seemed much greater on the moon than it was on earth. Earthbound, I would have stopped my run in just one step—an abrupt halt. I immediately sensed that if I did this on the moon, I'd be face down in lunar dust; I had to use three or four steps to sort of wind down. The same applied to turning around. Earthbound, it is a very direct motion; on the moon it is done in stages. My earth weight,

Aldrin walks on the moon. (*NASA*)

with the big back-pack and heavy suit, was 360 pounds. On the moon, in one-sixth of the earth's gravity, I weighed only 60 pounds.

We had a number of experiments to conduct and precious little time to do them. Because of the large variety of unknowns involved on this first trip, our surface activity was limited to two hours and forty minutes, and every minute was busy.

After all the gear and both of us were [back] inside, our first chore was to pressurize the LM cabin and to begin stowing the rock boxes, film magazines, and anything else we wouldn't need until we were connected again with the *Columbia*. Following that, we removed our boots and the big back-packs, opened the LM hatch, and threw these items onto the lunar surface.

We had a seven-hour rest period before beginning the final liftoff procedures and settled down for our fitful rest. I eased myself onto the small amount of available floor space while Neil leaned against the rear of the cabin and placed his feet in a small strap. We didn't sleep much at all. Among other things, we were elated—and also cold.

Liftoff from the moon, after a stay totaling 21 hours, was exactly on schedule and fairly uneventful. There was no time to sightsee. I was concentrating intently on the computers, and Neil was studying the attitude indicator. Three hours and ten minutes later we were connected once again with the *Columbia*.

The voyage to the moon was conducted within nearly half a second of the flight plan. Of all the various mid-course corrections it was possible to make en route to and from the moon, we had used only two. The training and preparation was such that even the unfamiliar surface of the moon was very nearly as we had been led to expect.

On the morning of July 24 [1969], nine days after we had left the earth, we began to re-enter the earth's atmosphere.

Biographical Notes

Edwin Eugene "Buzz" Aldrin, Jr. (1930–   ) flew the *Gemini 12* spacecraft to a rendezvous in orbit and flew *Apollo 11* to the first moon landing.

Henry Harley "Hap" Arnold (1886–1950), the senior pilot at Army headquarters during most of World War II, was chief of Army air forces during World War II.

Richard Evelyn Byrd (1888–1957) was the first man to fly over the north and south poles and organized several expeditions to explore Antarctica.

Michael Collins (1930–   ) "walked" in space from the *Gemini 10* spacecraft and flew the command ship *Columbia* during the first moon landing.

Benjamin Delahauf Foulois (1879–1967) became Army air chief in Europe during World War I and later chief of all Army air forces.

Virgil Ivan "Gus" Grissom (1926–1967) flew the suborbital *Mercury 4* spacecraft and orbited Earth aboard the first manned Gemini.

Francis Monroe "Frank" Hawks (1897–1938) taught Army students to fly during World War I and in later years set more than 200 speed records.

Ted William Lawson (1917–   ) piloted an Army B-25 on the World War II "Doolittle Raid," the only aircraft-carrier takeoff these planes ever made.

Curtis Emerson LeMay (1906–   ) led World War II strategic bombing, organized Strategic Air Command, then was chief of the U.S. Air Force.

Charles Augustus Lindbergh (1902–1974) was a parachutist, wing walker, barnstormer, and air-mail pilot before flying solo from New York to Paris.

Jacqueline Cochran Odlum was chief of Army female pilots during World War II and the first woman to fly faster than sound.

Amelia Mary Earhart Putnam (1898–1937) was the first woman to cross the Atlantic by airplane and the first woman to fly across it solo.

Edward Vernon Rickenbacker (1890–1973), top U.S. ace in World War I, spent 23 days in a raft after a World War II crash and later was an airline executive.

Floyd Herschel "Slats" Rodgers (1888–1956) survived years of barnstorming and retired to be a fishing guide in Texas.

Alan Bartlett Shepard, Jr. (1923–   ) was the first American into space and flew *Apollo 14* to become the fifth human to step onto the moon.

Dean Cullen Smith (1900–   ), an Army pilot in World War I before age 18, became an air-mail pilot and then joined Byrd's first Antarctic expedition.

Joseph Albert Walker (1921–1966) was an Army pilot during World War II and flew the X-15 as NASA's chief research pilot.

Orville Wright (1871–1948) was the first person to recognize that movable portions of each wing could control an aircraft's position in flight, a key discovery leading to the invention of the airplane with his brother Wilbur (1867–1912).

Charles Elwood "Chuck" Yeager (1923–   ), a World War II ace, was the first man to fly faster than sound and the first to fly at twice the speed of sound.

Bibliography
Aviators' First-Person Reports

Aldrin, Edwin E., Jr., with Wayne Warga. *Return to Earth.* New York: Random House, 1973.

Armstrong, Neil A., et al. *First On The Moon.* Boston: Little, Brown, 1970.

Arnold, Henry H. *Global Mission.* New York: Harper & Brothers, 1949.

Balchen, Bernt. *Come North with Me.* New York: Dutton, 1958.

Bridgeman, William, with Jacqueline Hazard. *The Lonely Sky.* New York: Henry Holt, 1955.

Byrd, Richard Evelyn. *Skyward.* New York: Putnam's, 1928.

Carpenter, M. Scott, et al. *We Seven.* New York: Simon and Schuster, 1962.

Cobb, Jerrie, and Jane Rieker. *Woman Into Space.* Englewood Cliffs, N.J.: Prentice-Hall, 1963.

Collins, Michael. *Carrying the Fire; An Astronaut's Journeys.* New York: Farrar, Straus and Giroux, 1974.

―――. *Flying to the Moon and Other Strange Places.* New York: Farrar, Straus and Giroux, 1976.

Crossfield, A. Scott, with Clay Blair, Jr. *Always Another Dawn.* New York: World, 1960.

Earhart, Amelia. *The Fun of It.* New York: Harcourt, 1932.

Everest, Frank K. *The Fastest Man Alive.* New York: Dutton, 1958.

Foulois, Benjamin D., with C. V. Glines. *From the Wright Brothers to the Astronauts.* New York: McGraw-Hill, 1968.

Grissom, Virgil I. *Gemini!* New York: Macmillan, 1968.

Hawks, Frank. *Speed.* New York: Brewer, Warren & Putnam, 1931.

———. *Once to Every Pilot.* New York: Stackpole Sons, 1936.

Irwin, James Benson. *To Rule the Night; The Discovery Voyage of Astronaut Jim Irwin.* Philadelphia, Pa.: A. J. Holman, 1973.

Lawson, Ted W. *Thirty Seconds Over Tokyo.* Robert Considine, ed. New York: Random House, 1943.

LeMay, Curtis E., with MacKinlay Kantor. *Mission with LeMay.* Garden City, N.Y.: Doubleday, 1965.

Lindbergh, Charles A. *Autobiography of Values.* New York: Harcourt Brace Jovanovich, 1978.

———. *The Spirit of St. Louis.* New York: Ballantine Books/Random House, 1974.

———. *"We."* New York: Putnam, 1927.

Mock, Jerrie. *Three-Eight Charlie.* Philadelphia, Pa.: Lippincott, 1970.

Odlum, Jacqueline Cochran. *The Stars at Noon.* Boston: Little, Brown, 1954.

Powers, Francis Gary, with Curt Gentry. *Operation Overflight.* New York: Holt, Rinehart and Winston, 1970.

Reichers, Lou. *The Flying Years.* New York: Henry Holt, 1956.

Rickenbacker, Edward V. *Fighting the Flying Circus.* Garden City, N.Y.: Doubleday, 1965.

———. *Rickenbacker.* Englewood Cliffs, N.J.: Prentice-Hall, 1967.

Scott, Robert Lee, Jr. *Boring a Hole in the Sky.* New York: Random House, 1961.

Smith, Dean C. *By the Seat of My Pants.* Boston: Atlantic–Little, Brown, 1961.

Stilwell, Hart, and Slats Rodgers. *Old Soggy No. 1.* New York: Messner, 1954.

Walker, Joseph A. "I Fly the X-15," *National Geographic Magazine,* September 1962.

Worden, Alfred M. *A Flight to the Moon* (I Want to Know About series). Garden City, N.Y.: Doubleday, 1974.

Wright, Orville. *How We Invented the Airplane.* Fred C. Kelly, ed. New York: McKay, 1953.

———. "Orville Wright: 'How We Made the First Flight,' " *The Wright Brothers,* Richard P. Hallion, ed. Washington, D.C.: Smithsonian Institution, 1978.

Yeager, Charles E. "Twice as Fast as Sound—I," in *The Saga of Flight.* Neville Duke and Edward Lanchbery, eds. New York: John Day, 1961.

Acknowledgments

John Gillespie Magee, Jr., "High Flight," quoted from the original manuscript on file at the Library of Congress.

Chapter 1: Excerpted and condensed from Orville Wright, deposition for defendant taken at Dayton, Ohio, January 13, 1920, detached from *Montgomery, et al.* v. *U.S.,* Court of Claims No. 33852, on file at Library of Congress, Papers of the Wright Brothers, Box 74.

Chapter 2: Excerpted and condensed from Benjamin D. Foulois with C. V. Glines, *From the Wright Brothers to the Astronauts.* Copyright © 1968 by Benjamin D. Foulois and C. V. Glines. Reprinted by permission.

Chapter 3: Condensed excerpt from *Global Mission,* by H. H. Arnold. Copyright 1949 by H. H. Arnold. Reprinted by permission of Harper & Row, Publishers, Inc.

Chapter 4: Adapted from *Fighting the Flying Circus* by Edward V. Rickenbacker. Copyright 1919 by David Edward Rickenbacker and William Frost Rickenbacker. Reprinted by permission of Doubleday & Company, Inc.